A note from the editor...

Well, this is it—the last month of Harlequin Temptation. We've had a good run, but everybody knows that all good things have to end sometime. And you have to admit, Temptation is very, *very* good....

When we celebrated our twentieth anniversary last year, we personified the series as a twenty-year-old woman. She was young, legal (well, almost) and old enough to get into trouble. Well, now that she's twenty-one and officially legal, she's leaving home. And she's going to be missed.

I'd like to take this opportunity to thank the countless number of authors who have given me, and other Harlequin Temptation editors past and present, so many hours of enjoyable reading. They made working at Harlequin an absolute pleasure.

I'd also like to thank our loyal readers for all their support over the past twenty-one years. Never forget—you are the reason we all do what we do. (Check out the back autograph section if you don't believe me.)

But this doesn't have to be the end....

Next month Harlequin Blaze increases to six books, and will be bringing the best of Harlequin Temptation along with it. Look for more books in THE WRONG BED, 24 HOURS and THE MIGHTY QUINNS miniseries. And don't miss Blazing new stories by your favorite Temptation authors. Drop in at tryblaze.com for details.

It's going to be a lot of fun. I hope you can join us.

Brenda Chin
Associate Senior Editor
Temptation/Blaze

Zack's self-control was crumbling fast

"I think it's time to say good-night, Gracie."

She leaned toward him and whispered, "Not yet."

He knew he'd lost the battle the moment her lips met his. His conscience tugged at him to stop, but Zack couldn't pull back now. Not yet. Not when she tasted so good. Not when his hands on her breasts evoked those soft, needy whimpers in the back of her throat.

Somewhere in a corner of his lust-fogged brain he knew this wasn't right, that making love to Gracie while impersonating Gilbert wasn't fair to her. But when he broke the kiss to tell her, she pushed him back on the bed, then slid one hand down to his waist and placed it over the bulge in his pants.

Zack groaned aloud. He was lost now. And he didn't care if he ever found his way back.

KRISTIN GABRIEL
GOOD NIGHT, GRACIE

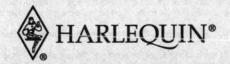

HARLEQUIN®

TORONTO • NEW YORK • LONDON
AMSTERDAM • PARIS • SYDNEY • HAMBURG
STOCKHOLM • ATHENS • TOKYO • MILAN • MADRID
PRAGUE • WARSAW • BUDAPEST • AUCKLAND

ISBN 0-373-69226-9

GOOD NIGHT, GRACIE

Dear Reader,

One of my favorite quotes is "A dream is just a dream. A goal is a dream with a plan and a deadline." (Harvey Mackay) We all have dreams, and my heroine, Gracie Dawson, is no different. But it's not until she turns her dream of seducing her best friend into a goal—with a plan and a deadline—that her life suddenly takes a turn in a new and exciting direction.

My goal in writing this latest installment of the fabulous WRONG BED miniseries was to make it both exciting and entertaining for my readers. I hope I succeeded.

I'd love to hear what you think about *Good Night, Gracie*. Please write to me at P.O. Box 5162, Grand Island, NE 68802-5162.

Happy reading—and may all *your* dreams come true!

Kristin Gabriel

Books by Kristin Gabriel

HARLEQUIN TEMPTATION

To all the wonderful authors of Harlequin Temptation—
thanks for the memories.

Prologue

"IT'S OVER."

The words she'd been dreading to hear rang in Gracie Dawson's ears. *It's over.* Her dreams of attending law school—of finally embarking on a life of her own—were over. Goliath had won again.

"I knew those biddies at the historical society would reject us." Cat Sheehan mixed drinks behind the mahogany bar while Cat's sister Laine sat shell-shocked on a bar stool between Gracie and waitress Tess Applegate.

As usual, the bar was empty of customers. Temptation was owned by the Sheehan sisters and housed in the same old brick building as Between the Covers, the bookstore Gracie had inherited from her aunt. Recent road construction had caused business to dwindle at both establishments, but that didn't make accepting their loss any easier.

This time Goliath had come in the form of city hall, with plans to demolish the building in order to widen the street. Appealing to the Kendall Historical Society to have the building declared a landmark had been their last hope.

Temptation was like a second home to Gracie and these women like a second family. She'd let them down. Just as she'd let down her aunt Fran, unable to challenge the insurance company that had refused to cover all the medical expenses incurred during her decade-long fight against kidney disease. They'd gone to lawyers for help, but none of them had been willing to take on the sprawling legal department of a huge corporation.

That made them gutless wonders in Gracie's estimation. She'd heard too many stories of people like her aunt at the mercy of bureaucrats and pencil-pushers. Gracie was ready to do some pushing herself—or shoving, as the case may be. But she needed a law degree first and that took time and money. Both would be in short supply now that she'd be forced to relocate the bookstore.

But she believed in loyalty—and keeping promises. Before her aunt had died, she'd told Gracie that as long as Between the Covers existed, a part of her would live, too. Gracie had vowed to keep her legacy alive.

She owed Aunt Fran that much.

Anger flared inside of her at the unfairness of it all. Her aunt had died eleven months ago, worn-out from the struggle of battling both the disease and the bill collectors whom she just managed to satisfy. She'd left everything to Gracie. The house. The bookstore. Her prized collection of Harlequin romance novels. Though she'd never married, Fran Dawson had been a romantic at heart.

Gracie had come to live with her in Kendall, Texas, when she was fifteen years old, after her parents had answered a call to become missionaries. Adjusting to life in Kendall had been difficult at first, made even more so by the tight cliques at her new high school. Losing herself in all those romance books had helped ease the transition.

So had Gilbert Holloway, the high school's resident computer geek, who had become her best friend. They'd spent most of their free time together watching vintage comedy shows on television and making big plans to attend the same college somewhere on the East Coast after graduation.

Then her aunt had been diagnosed with kidney disease and Gracie's plans had drastically changed. Chronically ill, Fran had depended on her for care and to help run Between the Covers. Gracie had never told anyone how much she'd missed going off to college like the rest of her classmates.

Just like she'd never told anyone how much she hated the bookstore.

Except for Gilbert.

He'd left for Boston after graduation and never looked back. For the past ten years, they'd corresponded almost daily by e-mail, his messages like a lifeline to her as her aunt's condition had worsened. He let her whine and rant and worry without judging her. Gilbert was the only man who understood her. The only man who knew how much her dreams meant to her.

Perhaps that's why she had so much trouble meeting men in Texas. Even while taking night classes over the past ten years to obtain her bachelor's degree, dates had been few and far between. None of the men she met ever lived up to Gilbert.

Maybe he was just safe. A man she could dream about without ever having to follow through. And dream she did, though Gilbert would never know about those fantasies. That was the *one* thing about her life that she didn't share with him.

Though she'd done plenty of looking, Gracie had never found a local version of Gilbert. She hadn't seen him in over a decade, but he was still the example she measured other men by.

Not that she'd done a lot of measuring lately. Running the bookstore didn't leave much time for a social life. This latest news meant putting everything in her life on hold indefinitely.

So be it. She wasn't about to surrender to the Goliaths of this world. Gracie Dawson would find a way to survive. She always did.

Laine visibly deflated beside her, making Gracie realize she'd only been thinking about herself. Temptation had been in the Sheehan family for over twenty years, handed down to the sisters by their mother, Brenda. Cat ran the bar while Laine worked full-time as a magazine photographer. They loved Temptation as much as she hated the bookstore.

"The city wants a new road, so we're out," Cat said, breaching the silence. She looked over at Gracie. "Did you really think we'd change anything tonight?"

Despite knowing it was a long shot, Gracie had

counted on it. Which was ridiculous, since nothing in her life ever turned out as she planned. At twenty-eight, she was certainly old enough to know that by now. It was time to start coping with reality.

"Where am I going to store all those books if I can't find a new place in thirty days?" she wondered aloud.

Nobody had any answers for her. Gracie knew she'd have to use every cent of her savings to make this move once she found a new location. A place that would undoubtedly charge higher rent for the bookstore than she was paying now. Add to that the advertising dollars needed to retain their old customers, as well as garnering new ones, and the task seemed overwhelming.

"How will I find another job as good as this one?" Tess asked. She'd hired on as a waitress a year ago, forming a fast friendship with Gracie, Cat and Laine.

Gracie wished she could offer Tess a position at the bookstore, but she'd be lucky to retain her assistant manager, Trina Powers, once they moved the store. Her budget had already been sliced and diced to the bare bones.

Laine looked up at her sister. "How are we going to explain this to Mom?"

Tess reached over and patted her hand. "Brenda will understand. She'll be pissed but she'll deal with it."

Angry tears gleamed in Laine's eyes. "I just can't believe it."

Cat pushed a cosmopolitan toward each of them. "Had faith in the system, Lainey dear?"

"Yes, I did," Laine replied, crushing the letter in

her hand. "This isn't right. How can they just take away everything we've worked for?"

"Because they can." Gracie took a sip of her drink, knowing this news had them all reeling—even Cat. She was just better at hiding it than the rest of them. They were at the mercy of the people in charge, powerless to change anything now.

She hated that feeling. That's why becoming a lawyer had been her dream for so long. She wanted to make a difference in peoples' lives.

Gracie watched Laine get up and turn away, making her wish she could have done something to make this situation turn out differently. It had been her idea to approach the Kendall Historical Society, hoping her exhaustive research into the history of the old building would sway them enough to name it a landmark. She'd handed it all over to Laine to make the presentation, but Gracie obviously hadn't given her enough ammunition.

Gracie slipped off the barstool and walked over to Laine, then put her arm around her shoulder. "This isn't your fault."

A bitter smile flickered on Laine's mouth. "Sure it is. If I'd talked to the right person, made the right argument…"

"It wouldn't have mattered. The city would still be steamrolling over our businesses."

"Maybe."

Gracie knew all too well how futile it was to imagine what might have been. You had to face life head-on and find a way to survive.

Her parents hadn't made it, succumbing to a jungle fever only six months after moving to South America. Neither had Aunt Fran. Gracie had survived through a lot of loss. But she was tired of just surviving. Tired of existing in limbo.

Now she wanted to live—*really* live.

"What are you going to do now?" Laine asked her.

"Find someplace cheap to lease for Between the Covers." Gracie looked around the bar at the oak paneling on the walls and the unique architectural detail on the high ceiling that matched that of the bookstore. "Whatever I find, it will never live up to this place."

"I've got money from my new job, if you need anything—"

"I'll be fine." Gracie knew she'd be able to handle the expenses by using her savings for law school. She'd been accepted at the University of Texas for the upcoming fall semester, but now that would never happen.

Maybe it was time to find a new dream.

Laine was watching Gracie, a mix of worry and self-recrimination in her eyes.

"You shouldn't take so much on yourself," Gracie told her, searching for some way to comfort her. "There's nothing more you can do here. Why don't you go away for a few days? Take some time for yourself."

Laine shook her head. "I can't. I just turned in my first assignment. I don't want it to be my last. Not to mention Aunt Jen is making me crazy. Those wild-fires in California are threatening…" her voice trailed off, then she looked up at Gracie. "June 30, right?"

"That's D-day apparently. Less than a month away."

Gracie's mind whirled with everything that needed to be done in that time. But she simply couldn't deal with it at the moment. Maybe she should take her own advice and get away from the bookstore for a few days. Her ten-year high school reunion was coming up this weekend in Kendall. That would be a perfect excuse to make a temporary escape from her responsibilities.

And a perfect excuse to fulfill the one dream she'd never dared to pursue.

1

ZACH MADDOX SAT illuminated in the blue glow of the computer screen. He'd been there for hours, cross-coding files and making another security sweep of the hard drive. At least, that was the excuse he was using to stay on the job. The reality was that he'd been waiting to hear from Gracie. He knew this was the day the decision was due from the Kendall Historical Society. He hoped her silence meant that she was out celebrating.

Yawning, he stretched his arms over his head, trying to ease the stiffness in his shoulders. He'd spent more time in this chair the past few months than he had in his own bed. Despite his efforts, they weren't any closer to discovering where Gilbert Holloway was hiding. The man had disappeared three months ago.

Holloway, a key witness in a conspiracy case involving credit card theft, had demanded police protection in return for his testimony. Closing his eyes, Zach wondered for the thousandth time why he'd let his partner stay alone with Holloway that night. The rookie had been determined to prove himself, but

Zach should have followed his instincts and pulled the duty himself.

That mistake had gotten Ray shot and cost him the use of his legs.

Some thug had broken in shortly before dawn, apparently to scare Holloway into silence. Ray had fallen asleep on the living room sofa. When he'd heard a window break, he'd panicked and pulled his gun before taking cover.

According to Ray's story, the thug had wrestled him for it while Gilbert escaped out the back door. The gun went off, wounding Ray and scaring the thug away. Zach still remembered coming in that morning to find his partner unconscious on the floor in a pool of blood.

The kid had taken a bullet in the back and it had been touch-and-go for a while. Long enough for Zach to feel out of control, a sensation he always did his best to avoid. So he turned his attention to something he could control—bringing the shooter in. He was certain Holloway could identify him—now he just had to find the guy.

Footprints in the dew-laden grass had led them to a neighbor's garage, where Holloway had apparently hot-wired a Jeep Cherokee before taking off to parts unknown. Three days later the Jeep had been found abandoned on a back road in southern Ohio, but there was no sign of Gilbert Holloway anywhere.

His best guess was that their star witness had staged a disappearing act for his own safety, not trusting the police to protect him anymore. Zach supposed he couldn't really blame the guy—though he thought Holloway was a bit of a wimp. One of those computer jockeys who lived, ate, and slept in front of a keyboard and monitor.

Like Zach was doing now.

At least he had a good reason. All of their leads had turned out to be dead ends. The only hope of finding Holloway now was connecting with one of his friends in cyberspace. Someone who might drop a clue as to where the man would hide.

It wasn't much to go on, but Zach didn't have any alternatives.

A ding resounded from the computer, signaling an incoming e-mail. Zach sat up straight in the chair, his pulse picking up speed.

Gracie.

His reaction had nothing to do with the case and everything to do with the woman on the other side of that e-mail. A friend of Holloway's from high school, the two of them had corresponded daily for the past ten years. After Holloway had disappeared, Zach had taken up the slack, pretending to be Gilbert. At first, he'd hoped to catch a break in the case, thinking Gracie Dawson might reveal something useful. After all, it seemed she knew the guy better than anybody.

But he soon discovered she knew nothing of Gilbert's foray into the criminal world. Zach should have stopped corresponding with her when he realized she couldn't help him locate Gilbert, but something kept drawing him to her e-mails. Something he couldn't quite pinpoint. Her witty, irreverent style? The way she made him laugh? Or maybe the loneliness he glimpsed between the lines. The same loneliness that engulfed him when he stopped working long enough to notice it.

He soon found himself caught up in the details of her life and in the woman herself. Zach knew how much she'd loved her aunt. How much she hated working at the bookstore. How long she'd dreamed of going to law school so she could become a plaintiff's attorney and fight all the injustices in the world.

A noble ambition. One that made him admire her all the more. Zach had tracked down an old high school yearbook in Gilbert's house to find her picture. He knew people changed over ten years, but she'd still have those same wide blue eyes. That same enticing smile.

He knew it was crazy to lust after a woman he'd never even met—one who lived over a thousand miles away. But maybe that's why she appealed to him.

Zach wasn't looking for a close relationship with a woman. He had seen too many fellow officers leave a wife and family behind to risk inflicting that kind of heartache on anyone. That's why he kept his relationships short-term, preferring to devote himself to his work. Everybody had to make choices in life.

Zach chose to go it alone.

He reached for the mouse, clicking on the e-mail. The subject line read *Plan B*. That wasn't a good sign.

Hi Gilbert,

I guess I'm not cut out to chase ambulances. Besides, who wants to graduate from law school when they're thirty-four years old? If you haven't guessed by now, the Kendall Historical Society turned down our application. So that means I'll have to find a new place for Between the Covers in the next twenty days and work there for approximately the next twenty years to pay off all the bills.

But no more whining. I promise.

Did you get your invitation to our high school reunion? Are you coming? It's been ten years since we've seen each other. That's much too long. I miss you, Gil, and I really need to see you.

Please say you'll be there.

Love, Gracie.

Zach read her e-mail again, feeling the pain behind her words. Giving up law school was killing her, no matter how she tried to brush it aside. Just last month she'd sent him an e-mail telling about her acceptance at the University of Texas. Her excitement had jumped off the computer screen.

Now she was in pain, though he knew she'd never reveal it to anyone else. Zach just wished there was some way to make her feel better. The same helplessness that had come over him in the hospital gnawed at him now.

Please say you'll be there.

Zach was so tempted. But how could he fly off to Texas when he had a job to do? Besides, she wanted to see Gilbert Holloway, not him. She didn't even know Zach existed.

He hit the reply button, then poised his fingers over the keyboard, hating the thought of causing her more disappointment. For a moment, he considered putting off a reply until tomorrow, but he didn't think he should give himself that time to mull over his response. His strong desire to see Gracie might overcome his better judgment.

Staring at the blank screen, he searched for the perfect words to let her down easy. At least she could commiserate with Cat, Laine, Tess and Trina. He'd read enough stories about them in her e-mails to make him feel as if he knew them all personally.

But Gracie was the one he saw when he closed his eyes at night. The one he made love to in his dreams.

"Just do it," Zach muttered to himself, hating any kind of procrastination. He believed in taking action, no matter what the consequences. That philosophy had saved his life on more than one occasion.

But as he started to type Gracie's name, a pop sounded from the computer and the screen went black, leaving him in total darkness. He rose from the chair and flipped up the light switch on the wall. Nothing. The electricity was off. What he didn't know yet was the reason why. A simple power failure or something more sinister?

Pulling his gun from his shoulder holster, Zach moved into the hallway. He didn't have a flashlight on him, but he knew the house well enough to navigate his way through the darkness and into the living room. Once there, light from the street lamps shone through the large picture window, illuminating his path. He could see the shadow of the bloodstain on the carpet where Ray had fallen—a daily reminder of how much was at stake in this investigation.

He cocked the gun, then moved into the kitchen. Two voices, both male, emanated from the garage. Zach stopped when he heard a door open into the house and leaned back against a cupboard.

"Yeah, it sucks, but at least we get overtime," said one of the men.

"Does overtime include the last four hours we spent at the bar watching the Red Sox?" asked the other.

"Hey, I'll earn a lot more than that if the Sox can win that thing. I've got a couple hundred bucks on 'em."

Zach holstered his gun. He recognized the voices and knew he wasn't in any danger. They belonged to the department's technicians, Shawn Foy and Jason Billings. Now he just had to find out what the hell they were doing here.

As the two men rounded the corner, the beam of a flashlight landed directly on Zach. They both jumped in surprise when they saw him.

"Damn," Shawn exclaimed. "You scared the crap out of me, Maddox."

"The lights were all off," Jason said. "We thought the house was empty."

"You were wrong." Zach held one hand in front

of his face to shadow it from the beam. "Turn that thing another direction before you blind me. Did you two shut off the electricity?"

"Sure did," Shawn replied. "We've got orders from Brannigan to close up the house and pack up all the equipment—including the computer."

Thomas Brannigan was Zach's commanding officer and in charge of the Holloway case. A veteran detective, he worked strictly by the book, which had caused more than a few skirmishes between the two of them. But he'd never done anything behind Zach's back before.

"Do you always work in the dark?" Zach asked, looking between the two of them.

Jason scowled. "It's not my fault. Shawn here thinks I'll turn on the ball game and leave him to do all the work."

"I don't think it, I know it," Shawn quipped. "That game was going into the fourteenth inning when I finally dragged him out of the bar. It's not worth losing my job over."

But Zach, once a rabid Red Sox fan, hadn't cared much about baseball over the past three months. All he cared about right now was solving this case. "Brannigan didn't say anything to me about moving the operation."

"We're not moving it," Jason said. "We're shutting it down."

Zach stared at him. "Like hell."

Shawn moved past him. "Sorry, Maddox, but we've got our orders. If you don't like it, you'll just have to talk to the boss. The sooner we get out of here, the sooner I can get back to the game.'"

Zach followed them into the small office and watched them unplug all the cables from the computer. He couldn't believe this was happening. Adding to his irritation was the fact that he hadn't gotten a chance to reply to Gracie's e-mail.

Certain there had to be a misunderstanding, Zach left the house and drove to Brannigan's home. The trip from Holloway's home on the south side of Boston took almost an hour. It was only when Brannigan answered his door wearing a robe and a scowl did Zach consider that he should have called first.

"Why the hell are you banging on my door at this time of night?" Thomas growled. "It sure as hell better be an emergency. My wife and kids are trying to sleep."

"We need to talk."

"Now?"

"It won't take long."

Brannigan's scowl deepened, but he opened the door wider and waved Zach inside. "Make it quick."

Zach crossed the threshold, almost tripping over a stuffed teddy bear in the foyer. Brannigan had four kids under the age of ten, a fact that was evident everywhere Zach looked. The toys littering the floor. The family pictures covering the wall. The cookie crumbs on the coffee table.

A sharp contrast to Zach's place, which barely had any furniture. Just a sofa, a bed, and a thirteen-inch television set. Not that he minded the Spartan environment, since he didn't spend much time there anyway.

"Well, get to it." Thomas tossed a Barbie doll off the sofa cushion before taking a seat.

"I heard a rumor that you're shutting down the Holloway case."

"It's no rumor," Thomas replied. "You know as well as I do that this case has reached a dead end. We can't afford to waste any more time on it."

Waste time? Zach was certain he couldn't be hearing him right. "So we just forget about it? Forget that Ray will never walk again? Forget that the scum who shot him is still out there somewhere?"

Brannigan's face hardened. "I'll never forget what happened to Ray. But you've been pushing the boundaries with this case ever since Ray got shot. I've given you some leeway, because he was your partner, but enough is enough. There are other cases to solve—other perps who need to be apprehended."

Zach rifled a hand through his hair, grappling for a way to change Brannigan's mind. His boss was a stubborn Irishman, but even he had to know this was a big mistake.

"You look like hell," Thomas said, scowling at him. "When was the last time you shaved?"

"Why the hell does it matter? I've been busy."

"You've been obsessed," his boss countered. "I tried to call you at home tonight to give you the news about the investigation, but I had to leave a message on your machine. You were sitting in front of that damn computer at the Holloway house again, weren't you?"

"That's my job," Zach reminded him.

"Don't give me that crap," Thomas spit out. "You're not on duty twenty-four hours a day. You've lost weight and look like you haven't slept in a week."

"Maybe if you worried as much about this investigation as you do about my appearance, we'd have found Gilbert Holloway by now."

Thomas slowly rose to his feet. "I've about had it with your attitude, Maddox. Don't push me."

But Zach didn't back off. "Hell, somebody's got to do it if we're ever going to find the bastard who shot Ray."

Thomas stared at him, a muscle twitching in his jaw. "I think it's time you took a vacation."

"I don't need a damn vacation. I just need to work this case."

"That's not going to happen. You're off the case and off the force for the next thirty days. Effective immediately."

His words were like a sucker punch to the gut. "You're suspending me?"

"Call it a mandatory vacation," Brannigan replied. "There's more to life than the job, Zach. You're going to burn out at this rate. You need to find yourself a beach somewhere in the Caribbean and start hunting for women instead of criminals."

He recognized that obstinate glint in Brannigan's green eyes. The man wasn't going to change his mind. Zach had gone too far this time.

"Now go home," Thomas ordered, ushering him

to the door, "and get some sleep. I don't want to see you for at least a month."

Before he could say another word, Zach found himself standing outside, the door slammed in his face. He'd blown it. Standing on the front porch, he replayed their conversation over in his mind, wondering if there was something else he could have said to convince Brannigan to change his mind.

It was too late now. He was off the case. But he had no desire to play beach bum for the next four weeks. There was only one place he wanted to go—one person he wanted to see. And the reasons why he should stay away didn't seem to matter anymore.

"Gracie Dawson, here I come."

2

THE NIGHT OF HER HIGH SCHOOL reunion, Gracie stepped into Between the Covers wearing her borrowed black dress and matching stilettos, feeling a little like Cinderella. Only she didn't intend to run away from her Prince Charming at midnight. Just the opposite, in fact.

She'd spent hours preparing for this night, grateful the reunion was in Kendall so she didn't have to factor in travel time. Yet, there was something pathetic about the fact that she hadn't left this place for the past ten years. Most of her classmates would be coming in from long distances.

"How do I look?" she asked her assistant store manager, turning in a slow circle.

"Sensational." Trina Powers walked out from behind the counter, the prosthesis on her left leg visible beneath her denim miniskirt. A motorcycle accident eight years ago had led to an amputation just above Trina's knee. Some days she used a wheelchair, but most of the time she wore the prosthesis, ignoring the stares of the customers and challenging anyone who tried to pity her.

Despite her disability, nothing ever stopped the thirty-two-year-old from performing her duties at the bookstore—or voicing her opinion.

"That's a Let's-Have-Sex outfit if I ever saw one," Trina said with a smile.

Gracie looked down at the slinky halter dress she had on loan from Tess. The four-inch heels belonged to Cat, who never seemed to have any trouble attracting men. "That's good because I'm definitely aiming for provocative."

"I know what we should do," Trina replied. "Let's ask the expert. Hemingway's around here somewhere."

Paul Toscano, an aspiring writer whom Trina had nicknamed Hemingway, was a daily fixture at the bookstore. Every morning he arrived with his laptop and a sack lunch, then settled into his favorite nook to work on his book-in-progress until closing time.

"Hey, Ernest," Trina bellowed, "come out here. We need your opinion on something."

Paul emerged from between the bookcases, pushing his wire-rimmed glasses up on his nose. His shirt and jeans fit loosely on his slight build and his auburn hair and beard were in need of a trim. His soulful brown eyes fixed on Trina and Gracie could see a blush form beneath his whiskers.

"You called?" he asked Trina.

"Gracie has a hot date tonight," Trina began, "and we need someone with a Y chromosome to tell us if this outfit she's wearing will trip his trigger."

His blush deepened as he turned his gaze to Gracie. "It's very nice."

Gracie wasn't going for nice. She wanted Gilbert's eyes to pop when he saw her. She wanted him to drag her up to his hotel room at the Claremont and ravish her. On second thought, *she'd* do the ravishing. After reading all those romances in her aunt's collection, she was ready to bring some of those erotic scenes to life.

"Nice?" Trina echoed, staring at Paul. "You're a writer. A wordsmith. Is that really the best you can do? How about sexy? Stunning? Irresistible?"

"Maybe I should take you with me to the reunion," Gracie said to her, "in case Gilbert needs some prodding."

"He won't," Paul said. "You look lovely."

Gracie wished she could be as confident. Gilbert hadn't responded to her e-mail, which wasn't like him. So she'd made a call to the reunion coordinator, who'd confirmed that he'd be there.

She took a deep breath, wondering what it would be like to see him again after all these years. Though there had been some gaps in his communications to her the past couple of years, he'd recently started e-mailing her more than ever.

Their exchanges seemed more personal somehow, with a sexual undercurrent that intrigued her, made her feel closer to him than ever. Maybe because they were both nearing thirty and still single. Whatever the reason, it was long past time to discover if their friendship could lead to something more.

"I looked Gilbert up in an old yearbook," Trina said, pulling one off the shelf. Between the Covers had every yearbook from Kendall High School dating back to 1934. "He's not exactly what I expected."

Gracie looked over Trina's shoulder as she paged to the senior picture section of the yearbook.

"There he is," Trina said, her finger tapping on his photo.

A stout teenage boy with shaggy dark hair, chipmunk cheeks and Coke-bottle bottom glasses that magnified his brown eyes stared back at Gracie. He wore a frayed denim jacket and a sullen expression, neither of which made him appear very appealing.

"Gilbert was never photogenic," Gracie said in his defense. "And he told me he lost a bunch of weight five years ago and had Lasik surgery, so the glasses are gone. Besides, I've gone out with plenty of guys who looked great on the outside but were jerks on the inside. At least I know Gilbert isn't a jerk."

"You're absolutely right." Trina closed the yearbook. "Besides, who am I to judge? It's not like I have a Gilbert or any other man knocking down my door."

Paul cleared his throat and started to say something, but before he could get the words out, Trina abruptly changed the subject.

"I found a couple of possibilities in the real estate section today." She moved to the counter and swiped the newspaper off the green marble top. "Not the best locations, but we obviously don't have time to be picky."

Gracie looked at the two items circle in red ink, guilt welling up inside of her. She hadn't given enough attention to their impending eviction, leaving all the work to Trina as she'd worked on the presentation to the historical society. That would change after this weekend. Then she'd make finding a new home for Between the Covers her first priority.

But right now all she could think about was Gilbert.

She wondered if he really had changed much physically since high school. Not that it mattered. He made her feel special and that was more important than a handsome face or a buff body. Still, a few doubts lingered in her seduction plan. What if the sparks simply weren't there? A wild weekend of hot sex wasn't worth ruining their friendship.

Was it?

The fact that she could even ponder such a question was proof that her long sex drought had taken its toll. Between running the bookstore and taking care of her sick aunt, Gracie hadn't been able to find much time for a social life.

"Here," Trina said, digging into her purse. "You'd better take these."

Gracie looked up from the newspaper to see Trina pull out a handful of colorful condom packages. Paul made a strangled noise in his throat at the sight of them.

"What?" Trina challenged, looking up at him. "You think a gimp can't get lucky?"

"You're not a…I never said…" Paul sputtered.

"Thanks," Gracie interjected, taking the condoms from her.

Why couldn't Trina see that the guy was totally in love with her? Or maybe she did see and just chose to ignore it. Paul wasn't exactly Mr. Exciting.

"Now go out and have fun," Trina said, propelling her toward the door. "And don't worry about the store. I can handle everything here."

"I'll help her," Paul said, then added quickly, "not that she needs it."

Trina laughed and Gracie was surprised by the pinprick of envy inside of her. She'd never had a man look at her the way Paul looked at Trina. The closest she'd come was in high school when Gilbert had asked her to the senior prom. She'd suggested they go out for pizza and bowling instead, fearing he'd only made the offer because she'd whined so much about not having a date. Now, ten years later, she was about to invite him to sleep with her.

She hoped it was an invitation he couldn't refuse.

ZACH STOOD IN THE BALLROOM of the Claremont Hotel wondering how he ever thought he could pull this off. The class of 1995 milled around him, their excited chatter punctuated by occasional shouts of recognition and giddy laughter.

He'd skipped his own high school reunion last year, where he no doubt would have felt as alien as he did now. Those days were a blur to him, mixed with unhappy memories of his father's abandonment when he was thirteen years old.

After he'd been made the man-of-the-house by default, Zach had given up sports and other school activities so he could go to work and help his mother keep their household afloat.

More than once, Zach had fallen asleep in class, exhausted from working double shifts at his job at the all-night delicatessen.

That was where he'd first considered a career in law enforcement, since it was a prime spot for the cruising patrolmen to take their breaks. He'd listened to their stories as he worked, enthralled by the excitement of it all. Compared to slicing salami and shredding lettuce, it had seemed like a dream job.

Now he knew that excitement came at a price. Like almost losing your partner. Or leaving a case unsolved. That still bothered him and he found himself scowling at the blond woman approaching him.

"Well, hey there," she said with a slight Southern drawl, "you don't look like you're having a very good time. Maybe I can fix that."

He pushed thoughts of the case out of his mind, forcing his face to relax into a smile. "I'm sure you can," his gaze dropped to the name tag on her ample chest, "Sandra."

She laughed. "You don't remember me, do you? Nobody's recognized me yet. I used to be a brunette back in high school. And a bit of a tomboy. Now, don't tell me your name. Let me guess."

He wondered how long it would take before she gave up, but he didn't mind waiting. Gracie hadn't shown up yet, so he had nothing better to do.

Sandra tilted her head to one side, looking him up and down. "You're Gilbert Holloway, aren't you?"

Zach blinked in surprise. He and Holloway were close to the same height and both had dark hair and eyes, but nobody would ever mistake them for twins. "How did you know?"

"Because I'm the official reunion greeter and the only two men who haven't picked up their name tags yet are Gilbert Holloway and Mitch Putnam." She laughed again. "But even with that Boston accent, I know you're not Mitch."

"Of course not," he agreed, wondering how she made the distinction. But he didn't want to blow his cover by asking. He was certain Gracie would realize he wasn't Gilbert as soon as she saw him. He just hoped she'd give him a chance to explain before revealing him as a fraud to everyone in the room.

Zach realized now that he'd been crazy to come here. Gracie wanted to see Gilbert, not him. She didn't even know him. Or realize that she'd been communicating with a complete stranger these past few months, telling him all her desires, spilling all her deepest secrets.

Making him fall in love with her.

Zach shook that unsettling thought from his head as soon as it appeared. He wasn't in love with her, just intrigued, maybe even infatuated. But that's as far as it went. That's as far as he'd allow it to go.

Despite his second thoughts, he'd come too far to back out now. Once he met Gracie and satisfied his curiosity, he could put her behind him. It might not be easy, but he'd done it before. All he wanted now was this one weekend with her. One weekend to fulfill the fantasies he'd had about her since her very first e-mail had touched something inside his soul.

Sandra peeled back the adhesive on Gilbert's name tag, then slapped it on his chest. "Can you believe how much everybody's changed? I wouldn't have recognized Stacie Winston if I'd passed her on the street and we started kindergarten together."

"A lot can happen in ten years," Zach replied, feeling more confident about pulling off this charade. Sandra didn't hesitate in accepting him as Gilbert Holloway.

Of course, he'd picked up on a few of the guy's mannerisms and speech patterns while acting as his bodyguard. Zach knew all Gilbert's favorite foods and little idiosyncrasies. And he'd read his journal, as well as all the e-mails exchanged between Gilbert and Gracie for the past decade, which were saved in a special file on Holloway's computer.

In some ways, he knew Gilbert better than he knew himself.

"I still can't believe it's been ten years since we graduated." Sandra leaned closer and lowered her voice. "Did you know Andy Winkleman's been married three times already? And Kendra Nebbles has four kids from four different men. I guess her parents shouldn't have forbidden her from taking that sex education class."

He knew all their names, having memorized them from the yearbook during his flight to Texas. Zach had treated this like any other undercover assignment, covering all his bases before he went into action. Only this assignment was personal and there was no set strategy—other than meeting Gracie.

He checked his watch, hoping he didn't have to wait much longer. "Do you know if Gracie Dawson's arrived yet?"

"Not yet." Sandra gave him a sly smile. "So tell me, were you two really just friends back in high school or was there more going on?"

That was a question Zach couldn't answer, so he hedged a little. "We've always been close."

She laughed. "And you've always been so secretive. I never could get any juicy tidbits out of you."

"I guess I'm just not a juicy kind of guy."

"Maybe not back in high school," she replied, her gaze roaming voraciously over his body. "But you have definitely improved with age."

Zach sensed it was time to move on, but before he could make an excuse to end their conversation, Sandra sidled closer to him.

"Can you believe it?" she asked in a hushed whisper, her gaze fixed across the room. "I think that's Allison Webb. Right over there, next to the punch bowl. Imagine her just showing up here like she graduated with all the rest of us! That certainly takes some nerve. Especially since I didn't even send her an invitation."

Zach followed her gaze and saw a tall blonde scoping out the room. "Did she drop out or something?"

Sandra looked up at him with a snort of disbelief. "How could you forget? It was the talk of the school for months. Allison just disappeared in the middle of our senior year. No warning. No explanation. Some people said she got pregnant. Others claimed she got busted for drugs and thrown in jail. But nobody ever knew for sure."

Now it clicked. In the back of the yearbook had been a mock-up of a wanted poster with Allison's picture on it and text underneath that read:

The senior class of Kendall High is offering a reward of one dollar for any information about AWOL classmate Allison Webb. She was last seen in the computer lab, wearing a pink sweater and white denim jeans.

"Well, it looks like the mystery will be solved tonight," Zach said. "All we have to do is ask her where she went and why."

Sandra smiled as she swept her arm in Allison's direction. "Be my guest, Mr. Holloway. I'll be waiting to soak up all your *juicy* tidbits."

Zach walked across the room, driven more by a desire to escape Sandra than any curiosity about Allison. As he approached her, she caught sight of his name tag, her eyes widening in surprise.

"Gilbert Holloway?" she said, looking him up and down.

"That's right," he replied. "How are you, Allison?"

"You know how I am." She moved closer to him and whispered, "The question is, what are you doing here?"

"Catching up with old friends," he replied, caught off guard by her reaction.

"Are you nuts?" she hissed. "This isn't the time to be playing games. There's too much at stake."

His instincts as a cop kicked into high gear at her words. It looked like there was more to the mystery of Allison than anyone here had imagined. There was something going on between her and Gilbert. Not a physical relationship, obviously, since she didn't realize he was an imposter—which left another incriminating possibility.

"I guess I like to live dangerously."

"I know why you're here," she accused, her gaze narrowing on him. "You want to see goody-two-shoes Gracie."

The jealousy in her tone was unmistakable. But he still couldn't be sure about her connection to Gilbert. He needed to draw her out and make her reveal something that would lead him in the right direction. "What makes you say that?"

"Maybe the fact that you're compromising the entire plan by showing up here tonight. Why did you insist that I make contact with Walker Mullen if you were planning to be here?"

Walker Mullen? The name didn't sound familiar. Just how many alumni from the class of '95 were involved in this case?

"In case you're interested, he bought my story about the stalker and is making the plans for us to travel incognito. I'm supposed to pick up the airline tickets at his agency on Monday."

So Walker Mullen was a local travel agent—and a dupe. That answered one question but still didn't get him any closer to finding Gilbert.

"Now you're taking a chance of blowing everything. And for what?" She rolled her eyes. "A chance to moon over Gracie Dawson?"

Zach wished he knew what she was talking about. He was floundering here and had no idea how to dig for more information without revealing himself.

"Let me buy you a drink," he offered, noting the empty glass in her hand. He could smell the alcohol on her breath and hoped a little more would help her loosen her tongue.

She shook her head. "I'm leaving now. Besides, I prefer to keep a clear head. It's safer that way. And I suggest you do the same—especially around Gracie. If she gets in the way…"

"What?" he prodded, his skin prickling at her tone.

"Just follow the plan and Gracie won't get hurt," Allison replied. "I know where she lives, so if anything goes wrong—and I mean, anything, then she'll be the one who pays. Got it?"

Before he could reply to her not-so-veiled threat, Allison turned on her heel and walked away. Zach started to follow her when another woman came into his view. The woman he'd flown over a thousand miles to meet. The woman he'd only seen before this moment in a yearbook and in his dreams.

Gracie.

3

GRACIE STOOD in the crowded ballroom at the Claremont Hotel, her gaze skimming over the faces of her old classmates. Some were familiar to her, some she barely recognized anymore. A few of them cast glances her way, but most were engaged in conversation, gathered in small clusters at tables or standing around the bar.

The one classmate she didn't see was Gilbert. Her heart sank when she realized all her preparation—the dress, the shoes, the romance books, just might have been for nothing. It looked like Gilbert was a no-show. Maybe her e-mail had sounded too desperate, too needy. She'd scared the man off. That was probably the reason he'd never bothered to reply to her.

Gracie walked over to the punch bowl, telling herself not to obsess about it. She could still have a good time tonight and reacquaint herself with all of her old classmates—although the thought of hearing all of their success stories depressed her even more.

"Gracie Dawson, is that really you?"

She turned around to see a buxom blonde barreling down on her. The woman held a name tag in one hand and a margarita in the other. Her face looked somewhat familiar, but Gracie couldn't place her.

"You don't know who I am, do you?" the woman said, laughing as she slapped the name tag onto Gracie's dress. "It's me, Sandra Atley. And here I thought geeky Gilbert would win the award for Most Changed Since High School."

"Geeky Gilbert?" she echoed, her heart skipping a beat. "Is he here?"

"Of course he's here," Sandra replied. "And wait until you see him. You won't believe your eyes." She grabbed Gracie by the elbow and pivoted her around. "He's right over…" Her voice trailed off and she frowned. "Well, he *was* right over there. I'm not sure where he is now."

Gracie smoothed down her dress and tried not to hyperventilate, aware that he could appear at any moment. "So how have you been, Sandra?"

"Fantastic," she replied. "I just got transferred to the Kendall State Bank from the main branch in Houston. It's great to be back home again. I'm still a teller, but I've got my eye on a management position. It's all about networking, you know, and I've already scored some great dirt on the current bank manager."

Gracie forced herself to maintain eye contact instead of looking around for Gilbert. *Let him come to me.*

"So what about you, Gracie?" Sandra asked. "Are you married? Any kids?"

"Oh, no," Gracie replied. "Not yet, anyway. The bookstore keeps me too busy."

Her smile softened with pity. "Are you still working there? It's such a sweet little place. I heard about your aunt passing away and meant to send you a card, but time got away from me. That's why I'm so excited to be moving back to Kendall. Everything in the big city is just rush, rush, rush!"

"So I've heard." Gracie didn't know what else to say, reminding her of how little she'd had in common with most of her classmates at Kendall High. She'd thought ten years might have changed that, but a quick perusal of the ballroom showed that many of the old cliques still remained, though the lines were a bit more blurred now.

She'd always been an outsider, along with Gilbert. Now she wanted to find him again and see if the bond they'd shared a decade ago was still there. A bond that had grown even stronger these past few months. He seemed more thoughtful in his e-mails now. Less cynical. Though he still had the ability to make her laugh.

She wouldn't be surprised if she was the one who had really changed, especially since Aunt Fran's death. After working through her grief, she'd become more driven than ever to pursue her dream to become a lawyer. Not that she'd ever succeed now— but Gilbert had always believed in her.

And that had made all the difference in the world.

"There's Honey Tate." Sandra pointed across the ballroom. "Rumor has it that she's marrying some senile oil tycoon from San Antonio. Remember how she was always flirting with all the male teachers in school? Looks like she was polishing her skills for the geriatric set."

"I don't recognize half the people here," Gracie said, still amazed at the changes in some of her classmates. She wondered if she looked as different to them as they did. Her hair was shorter than it had been in high school and she'd gained a few pounds. Though she'd skipped the boob job that had dramatically altered Sandra's appearance.

"Who is that over by the palm tree?" Gracie asked.

"Mitch Putnam," Sandra replied. "Isn't it a hoot? The guy's at least six inches taller than he was in high school. He must have gotten lifts or something."

"Maybe he just had a late growth spurt."

"It's certainly possible." Sandra adjusted her cleavage. "That's what happened to me." Then she dug her arm into Gracie's ribs. "Don't look now, but here he comes."

"Mitch?"

"No, Gilbert!"

Gracie's breath caught in her throat as she turned to see a man approaching them. But as soon as she saw him she realized it wasn't Gilbert. This man was too handsome. Too confident. Too...sexy.

Despite her disappointment, she couldn't take her eyes off him. She barely heard Sandra's whispered plea to put in a good word for her before she found herself standing alone with him.

"Hello, Gracie."

The way he said her name sent a shiver of awareness down her spine and she forced her gaze from
his dark brown eyes to the name tag on his jacket.

Gilbert Holloway.

Her gaze flicked to his face again and she searched
for some hint of familiarity. But without all that
weight, and those glasses that had distorted his face,
he looked like a stranger.

"I can't believe it's you," she breathed, still staring up at him.

"I can't believe how beautiful you look tonight."

His voice had changed, too, deeper now and more
resonant. The boy she'd known had become a man
in the past ten years. A sexy, virile, irresistible man.

"I don't know what to say," she sputtered, realizing she'd already blown her plan to be cool and al-
luring. She was gaping like an idiot and no doubt
sounding like one, too.

"Then don't say anything. Dance with me?" he
asked, holding out his hand.

She grasped it, relishing the way his broad fingers
closed around hers. He led her onto the small dance
floor, then pulled her into his arms.

Gracie was still in shock, but she managed to
avoid stepping on his toes.

"We're finally together again," she said, "after all
this time."

"Finally," he agreed, drew her even closer until
her head rested against his shoulder. The old Gilbert
had always smelled like pepperoni, due to his daily
diet of frozen pizza. This new Gilbert carried the

aroma of musk and man, an erotic combination that almost made her dizzy.

"When did you get here?" she asked, trying to regain her equilibrium. This was just Gilbert, after all. Her oldest and dearest friend. There was no reason for her heart to be tripping in her chest this way or for her knees to feel weak.

"My plane arrived in Dallas this morning and I drove a rental car from the airport."

"How was your flight?" Another stupid, mundane question, but she was still trying to wrap her mind around the fact that Gilbert was here, in her arms, and more incredible than she'd ever imagined.

"Fine. I slept most of the way."

She smiled up at him. "Slept? Does that mean you don't have anxiety attacks at thirty thousand feet anymore?"

He hesitated, then gave a short nod. "People change."

That was the understatement of the millennium. But Gracie wasn't going to question it, not when this reunion had turned out better than she'd ever imagined.

She swayed to the music, feeling like she was born to be in his arms. "Where did you learn to dance like this?"

A smile kicked up one corner of his mouth. "The Internet."

"No, really."

His smile widened. "It's the truth. I always wanted to learn how to dance, but never had the time. So I used a search engine to locate online dance lessons."

"Online dance lessons," she echoed, still skeptical. "Nobody learns to dance like this all by themselves."

"I might have honed my skills at a few clubs on the weekends."

His admission evoked a pang of envy at the thought of another woman in his arms. A ridiculous reaction, since they hadn't seen each other for ten years. The new-and-improved Gilbert had no doubt slept with countless women. He probably had to turn them away at his bedroom door.

But he wouldn't be turning Gracie away—not if she had anything to say about it. She even had a backup plan tucked away in her purse, in case he needed a little prodding in the right direction.

The thought of sleeping with him sent a shiver of uncertainty through her. Before, she'd envisioned the shy, gawky Gilbert from her high school days, a man who might be as inexperienced as she was between the sheets. But something told her that he was as good a lover as he was a dancer. No doubt another skill that he'd perfected over the years, and not from any online lessons.

She hoped he wouldn't be disappointed—if they got that far. Maybe she needed to rethink this plan before she made a complete fool of herself.

The music ended, but Gilbert didn't release her from his embrace. "Shall we find a table and have a drink or keep dancing?"

As much as she'd enjoyed their dance, Gracie

needed a few moments alone to refocus. "A drink sounds good to me. Would you mind getting me a glass of champagne while I make a dash to the ladies' room?"

"Not at all," he replied. "Shall we meet at a table by the atrium?"

"See you there." Gracie watched him walk away, then took a deep breath as she went in search of a restroom. She found one in the lobby, enjoying the brief respite from the music and milling crowd to get her head together.

She walked inside the ornate restroom, the sinks and stalls on one side and a plush lounge area on the other. As she headed to a sink, she recognized two former cheerleaders from Kendall High, Carol Ann Blume and Mitzi Mobley. They sat on a suede sofa together talking, unaware or unconcerned of her presence.

Just like back in high school.

Gracie smiled to herself, remembering how much their behavior would have wounded her then. Now she had much bigger things to think about. The biggest at the moment being the man waiting for her in the ballroom. The man she planned to seduce tonight.

She pulled a paper towel from the dispenser, running it under cold water, then wringing it out before pressing it to her flushed face. As Gracie stood at the sink, part of their conversation caught her attention.

"Did you get a look at Gilbert Holloway?" Mitzi asked her companion.

"Oh, I know!" Carol Ann exclaimed. "Talk about a transformation."

"The guy went from geek to Greek god. Makes me wish I'd been nicer to him back in high school."

Carol Ann laughed as they got up and headed for the door. "Makes me wish I'd left my husband at home tonight!"

Gracie pulled the paper towel from her face, then touched up her makeup. As she applied her lipstick, she became more determined than ever. Gilbert might have changed on the outside, but he was still the same sweet guy on the inside.

So she didn't need to be intimidated by him. He was the guy who used to sing show tunes to her when she was feeling down. The same guy who had cried watching *Schindler's List*. Women like Sandra, Carol Ann and Mitzi would never appreciate his inner qualities.

Which meant she'd be crazy to miss this opportunity to take her friendship with Gilbert to the next level.

Refreshed and resolved, she walked out of the restroom and into the ballroom. She looked toward the atrium and saw Gilbert already seated at a table. Sandra stood on the other side of him, leaning just far enough in his direction to give Gilbert an R-rated view of her surgically bloated breasts.

"We were just talking about you," Sandra trilled as Gracie approached the table.

"Really?" She took a chair right next to Gilbert, then smiled up at Sandra. "You're such a dear. Thanks for keeping Gilbert company while I was gone. I can take over from here so you can go have some fun."

Disappointment flashed in Sandra's pale blue

eyes, but she hid it with a wide smile. "It was my pleasure. I'll see you two later."

"Bye," Gracie said, watching Sandra turn and head in the direction of another lone male. Then she reached for her champagne, suddenly aware that Gilbert might have been enjoying Sandra's little peep show. "I hope I wasn't interrupting anything."

"You're amazing," he said, turning to look at her. "You got rid of Sandra, but did it in such a polite way that she thanked you for it."

"That's called Southern manners. Also known as slopping sugar. Surely you haven't been away from Texas for so long that you don't remember how it works?"

He smiled. "I guess I just needed a refresher course. I'm a long way from home."

"Is Boston really so different from here?"

He met her gaze. "It's like another world."

When he looked at her like that, Gracie felt like they were the only two people in the ballroom. She found herself wishing she could read his mind. That she could know for certain this desire sizzling inside of her wasn't completely one-sided.

"By the way, I want to apologize for never responding to your last e-mail," he said. "I've been having some computer problems."

That made her feel better. "To tell you the truth, I wasn't sure you'd be here tonight."

"I should have called you," Gilbert admitted. "But I wanted it to be a surprise. I hope you don't mind."

"Not at all." Gracie drained her glass, sensing that

it was now or never. If she didn't make her move, she'd chicken out. But despite that she'd rehearsed this moment a hundred times in the last few days, Gracie couldn't make herself say the words. Coming face-to-face with Gilbert, a man she didn't even recognize anymore, was completely different than propositioning his picture in the yearbook.

So she settled for her backup plan.

"You're full of surprises lately," she said, setting the empty glass on the table. "I love the present you sent me."

He arched a dark brow. "Present?"

"Last week. The video." Gracie reached into her purse and pulled it out, almost spilling the condoms onto the floor. She hastily stuffed them back inside, hoping he hadn't noticed.

Gilbert didn't say anything, making her even more nervous.

"I brought it along in case the reunion got boring and we wanted to bail out and go watch it together," Gracie said, aware she was talking too fast. "You know, like old times?"

She wanted to sink into the floor. It sounded so lame. And transparent. They weren't in high school anymore. Gilbert spent his Saturday nights in clubs now, not watching old reruns on television.

His silence stretched into an eternity. Then he took the videotape out of her hands. "How about watching it right now? I think I have a VCR in my hotel room. I bet we can even order a pizza from room service."

"Pepperoni?" she said, relieved that he hadn't

rejected her offer. That's when Gracie realized just how much this night with Gilbert meant to her. She'd been alone for so long.

He grinned. "Is there any other kind?"

She looked around the crowded ballroom. "Would it look bad if we left this early?"

He tipped her chin up with one finger until her gaze met his. "I'm looking at the only person I came here to see."

Gracie's breath caught at the raw desire she saw in his brown eyes. So maybe the attraction wasn't one-sided, after all. That very real possibility both excited and terrified her at the same time.

"I suppose it will be fitting," she said, trying to lighten the moment, "since we skipped the graduation dance and watched old comedy shows on TV all night."

He smiled. "Then let's say good night, Gracie."

It was his signature line, the one that had always ended their telephone conversations in high school and his e-mail communications since then. For the first time since he'd appeared in the hotel ballroom, the man beside her seemed less like a stranger and more like the old friend she remembered.

Feeling more relaxed now, Gracie let him lead her out of the ballroom to the bank of elevators that would take them to his room. But she didn't plan to say good-night to Gilbert anytime soon.

If Gracie had anything to say about it, their night was just beginning.

4

ZACH HAD RESISTED his share of temptations on the job—like free merchandise offers from vendors seeking special treatment from the Boston P.D. and sexual propositions from women with kinky fantasies about a man in uniform. But none of them had even begun to compare to the temptation standing next to him now.

He slipped his key card into the hotel room door, his duty as a cop battling with his needs as a man. Gracie was everything he'd expected—and more. Not only was she a knockout, she was as genuine in person as she'd been in all of her e-mails—and so damn sexy he'd hardly been able to walk off the dance floor.

"After you," he said, holding the door open for her.

Zach inhaled the exotic aroma of her perfume as she walked past him, his gaze drawn to the enticing sway of her hips in that killer dress. He followed her inside, letting the door fall closed behind him.

He was in dangerous territory now.

Unfamiliar territory, too. He'd never lied to a

woman about his identity before. Now he found himself forced to continue to play the part of Gilbert Holloway. Deceiving everyone down in that ballroom had been innocent fun. But deceiving Gracie… Zach sucked in a deep breath, knowing he didn't have any other choice.

Especially now that the Holloway case had just been blown wide-open. The discovery of Allison Webb's connection to Gilbert, followed by Gracie's revelation that she'd received a gift from the guy last week made it impossible for Zach to reveal his identity. Not when he'd just been handed his first real lead in this case.

When Gracie had pulled that videotape out of her purse, it had been like a bomb had gone off in his head. The events of the past few months has swirled together in a chaotic whirlwind of memories. Ray unconscious and bleeding on the floor. Holloway's vanishing act. The long nights in front of the computer, searching for a break in this case.

Now, in the space of an hour, he'd had two clues land right in his lap. Zach tried to tell himself that the videotape might not mean anything, that it could be just an innocent gift from one friend to another. But his gut told him a different story. Holloway was on the run and wouldn't take the chance of making contact with Gracie unless it was important. Important enough to risk his life.

Judging by Allison's hostile reaction down in the ballroom, Gracie's life, or at least her safety, was also at risk. Zach's appearance as Gilbert at the reunion might have set something in motion that could prove dangerous to her. He was already responsible for one person getting hurt on this case. He damn well wasn't about to allow it to happen again. That gave him another reason to stay close to Gracie.

The king-size bed dominated the room and Zach's pulse picked up when Gracie sat down on it and crossed her legs. She probably had no idea how provocative she looked, with her stiletto heel dangling from one slender foot, how the shapely curves of her long legs sparked a primitive reaction inside of him.

At this moment, he wanted nothing more than to strip off her dress and pull her down on top of him to assuage the ache inside of him that had grown with each one of her e-mails over the past three months and each one of her smiles this evening.

But he couldn't take advantage of Gracie that way. Not when she thought he was Gilbert Holloway. So he corralled his lust, ignoring the heavy throb in his groin as he moved toward the bed.

"Shall we order the pizza first?" he asked.

"I'm not really hungry." She leaned back on the bed, her arms braced behind her. The angle highlighted the long curve of her neck and the creamy skin below. The slinky fabric of her dress molded against her breasts and outlined two perfect, pert nipples. "Are you?"

Zach stared, mesmerized. His willpower was quickly flagging and he couldn't remember the question. "What?"

A smile teased her pink lips, her tongue peeking out to moisten them. He almost groaned aloud, his hands curling into fists. Bringing her to his hotel room had been a bad idea. A very bad idea.

"I'm not really that hungry now," she repeated. "Are you?"

Hell, yes, he was hungry. Ravenous, in fact. He wanted to devour every inch of her, starting with her mouth and moving down her soft, supple body one delectable inch at a time.

When he reached her breasts, he'd take his sweet time, savoring each one. Then he'd move lower, tasting her. Driving her wild. Just like she was doing to him now.

"Gilbert?" she said, her brow crinkling at his long silence.

Zach collected himself. "Hungry? No, not really." Then he swept the videotape from the bed. "So why don't we skip the pizza and start the show."

"Sounds good to me," Gracie said. "Do you mind if I get more comfortable?"

If she got any more comfortable he was going to explode. He tried to ignore the incessant throbbing in his groin, telling himself this was his penance for lying to her. "Go right ahead."

She smiled, then kicked off her stilettos. They both hit the wall with a bang. "Those shoes were killing me."

He breathed a long sigh, both grateful and disappointed that her shoes were all she wanted to remove. Then she stood up and proved him wrong. Gracie lifted the hem of her dress to the top of one thigh, revealing a lacy black garter underneath.

His mouth went dry as she popped open the snaps, the sound reverberating inside of him. He watched her slide the silk stocking down her long leg. Her movements so slow and seductive that he could hear the rapid beat of his pulse inside his ears. Time stood still as she moved to the other leg, popping the snaps on that garter, then removing it along with the second stocking.

"There," she said, straightening to her full height. "That's much better."

Zach turned to the television set to insert the videotape into the VCR, grateful for a few moments to gather himself and figure out how to breathe again. He fiddled with the buttons for a while before finally pushing the play button.

"Here we go," he said, adjusting the volume with the remote control. Now he could focus his attention on this case instead of Gracie. All he had to do was keep his eyes on the television set.

Music from the introduction to the old Burns and Allen show filled the room. Taking a deep breath, he turned around to find Gracie propped on a pillow against the headboard.

She tossed him the other pillow, then patted the empty space beside her. "There's plenty of room here for the two of us. Certainly more room than that old love seat we used to share in your basement."

Jealousy, hot and swift, rose up inside of him at the thought of her cuddling with Holloway on a love seat. He knew they'd never been intimate, having read Gilbert's journal about all the missed opportunities he'd had with Gracie. The guy had been seriously conflicted, lusting after his best friend but too insecure about his weight and his masculinity to do anything about it.

At the time, he'd felt a little sorry for the guy. Now he could only be happy that Holloway hadn't acted on his desires, a feat even more difficult than Zach had imagined now that he found himself in a similar situation.

He took the pillow, but placed it on the foot of the bed, then stretched out onto his stomach, his head even with Gracie's bare feet. He tried to focus on the show, looking for any clue that might lead him to Gilbert, but when the mattress shifted and Gracie joined him at the foot of the bed, he knew he was lost.

He could smell the aroma of lilacs in her hair. Feel the warmth of her body so close to his own. Hear the soft laughter in her throat as she watched the show. The minutes stretched into an eternity as he found himself covertly watching her more than the videotape. Yet all too soon, the music flared and his gaze flicked to the television to see the credits roll across the screen.

Zach swallowed a sigh of relief. He'd made it. His willpower had conquered his desire for her, though it had been a close call. A *very* close call. He didn't dare move off the bed and reveal the arousal that would be all too apparent through his dress slacks. Instead he turned to her, surprised how close she was.

He sucked in a deep breath. If she didn't leave

in the next thirty seconds, his self-control was going to crumble. "I think it's time to say good night, Gracie."

She stared at him for a long moment. Then she leaned toward him and whispered, "Not yet."

He knew he'd lost the battle the moment her lips met his. He surrendered with a moan of anticipation that got lost in the sweet cavern of her mouth. It echoed deep within him as her sweet, sultry kiss filled the void that had ached inside of him for so long.

His conscience tugged at him to stop, but Zach couldn't pull back now. Not yet. Not when she tasted so good and leaned into him that way. Not when his hands on her breasts evoked those soft, needy whimpers in the back of her throat.

Somewhere in a corner of his lust-fogged brain, he knew that this wasn't right, that making love to Gracie while impersonating Gilbert wasn't fair to her. But when he broke the kiss to tell her, she pushed him back on the bed, then slid one hand down past his waist and placed it over the bulge in his slacks.

Zach groaned aloud, knowing he was lost now and didn't care if he ever found his way back. Her fingers moved over him, tentative and exploring. He closed his eyes, letting her set the pace and enjoying every second of it. She stroked the long length of him and he moaned aloud at the sensation. Then she replaced her hand with her mouth, working it up and down over the fabric of his slacks.

He almost lost control at the warm contact. Not ready for this real-life fantasy to be over, he pulled her up to him and kissed her with a need that almost scared him.

There had never been a woman like this before. No one who had driven him to this point of desperation. But Zach needed more than her body. He wanted part of her soul, a connection that would fill him completely.

She broke the kiss, then reached up to untie the knot at her nape, letting the bodice of the dress fall to her waist. No bra obscured his view as he gazed at her two luscious breasts, the nipples pink and pouting for his attention.

He just stared for a moment, watching her breasts rise up and down with her rapid breathing. Then her eyelids fluttered shut as he bent forward and flicked his tongue across one nipple, savoring the texture. She moaned deep in her throat, her body arching up to give him better access.

Like a banquet set before him, Zach laid her back on the bed, then settled in to enjoy the feast. She tasted even better than he'd imagined, her skin sweet and slightly salty as his tongue circled one nipple, then the other. They beaded under his mouth, and he saw her hands clench and unclench the bedcover as her body shuddered with need.

"Please," she murmured, leaving her wishes unspoken. But he knew instinctively what she wanted.

He wanted it, too.

Zach trailed kisses down her soft belly, slowly pushing her dress lower with his hands. She writhed on the bed, crying out when he reached the top of her black panties. He hovered there, drawing out the moment until she threaded her fingers in his hair and urged him to the essence of her.

Sliding his tongue over the hot, moist silk of her panties, Zach settled in for another feast. When she began to move against his mouth, he bracketed her hips with his hands, slowing her movements.

"Oh, please," she rasped, grabbing the headboard above her. "Don't stop."

He had no intention of stopping. But Zach had come too far and waited too long for this to end now. He wanted it to last all night. So he turned his head and dropped kisses on the tender skin of her inner thigh until her breathing slowed a bit. The combination of her cries and her scent soon drove him back to her panties again and he used his tongue to drive her wild once more.

"Wait," she gasped when she couldn't take it anymore, half sitting up on the bed.

He drew back, slipping the dress off her body in one fluid motion. She reached out for him, and pulled off his jacket, then his shirt and tossed them both to the floor.

He forced himself not to move when her hands settled on his belt and her fingers undid the buckle, brushing his arousal. Soon his belt was off, followed by his slacks and boxer shorts. He stood naked before her, his body taut and ready.

She wore only her panties, but left them on as she reclined on the bed once more and held her arms out toward him. This was the point of no return. But

Zach couldn't resist her invitation any more than he could stop breathing. He lay on top of her, his arousal sliding against the silk of her panties.

Gracie wrapped her arms around his neck, arching up against him. The friction of their bodies moving together almost undid him, but he held on long enough to become aware of the condom she'd placed in his hand. It was already unwrapped, making it a simple matter of rolling it onto his erection.

Or not so simple, he thought when she took over the task herself. What had always seemed like a chore now became one of the most erotic acts he'd ever experienced. Gracie used her hands and her tongue to bring him to the brink and back again.

Zach pulled her down on the bed, knowing he couldn't hold on much longer but determined to give her just as much pleasure as she was giving him. He slid her panties down to her ankles, leaving them there to prevent her from opening her legs for him too soon. She seemed to relish the silk bondage, her moans growing louder as his hands delved into the curls at the junction of her thighs.

He took his time, glad he still retained a thin thread of control that allowed him to explore her body. He watched her face when his fingers found the hot, moist center of her desire. She arched on the bed as he circled the tiny bud, her eyes closed and her lips parted. Zach wanted to watch her come to completion, but she refused to go alone.

After kicking off her panties, Gracie encircled his thighs with her legs, then drew him down on top of her. As his arousal penetrated the silken folds of her flesh, they both cried out, then moved in a primitive rhythm that neither one of them could control.

His climax came much too soon, washing over him at the same time that she screamed out a name. But not his name.

Gilbert.

He sunk on top of her, burying his face in the hollow of her neck as spasms racked both of their bodies. She clung to him, her arms and legs entwined around him until he didn't know where he ended and she began. It had been perfect.

Almost.

Gilbert. The name echoed in his ears and left a sour taste in his mouth. Afraid he was crushing her, Zach rolled to his side, taking her with him.

He was determined not to let that name ruin this moment. Zach was the one holding her. He was the one she leaned up to kiss now, a soft blush blossoming on her cheeks.

"It was definitely worth waiting ten years for you," Gracie said huskily, tears shimmering in her beautiful blue eyes. "I'll never forget this night."

Zach didn't know what to say. He certainly couldn't tell her the truth now. He could barely put two words together after what had just happened between them. It had been more than sex, more than lust. His reaction was something he'd never had with any woman before. Ever.

Worst of all, he'd barely put up a fight. Zach Maddox, who prided himself on his self-control, had wilted under her touch. But that didn't mean he regretted making love to her. On the contrary, he wanted it to happen again. And again.

But not until she knew the truth.

He wasn't sure how to tell her yet and now certainly wasn't the moment to do it. But Zach wasn't a man to run from a challenge. And he sure as hell wasn't going to run from Gracie Dawson.

She needed him to protect her, even if she didn't know it yet, at least until he found Gilbert and the rest of his partners in crime. Now he just had to figure out how to do that without complicating her life even further.

But thought was impossible with Gracie lying in his arms. His eyelids grew heavy and he felt more relaxed than he had in years. Zach told himself he'd figure it all out tomorrow, when he had time to make her understand.

She needed to know the truth about him so she could call out *his* name the next time they made love. And there would be a next time—Zach had no doubt about that.

Because he wasn't about to let Gracie go.

5

FOR THE FIRST TIME that Gracie could remember, the reality was better than the dream. She lay beside Gilbert the next morning, watching him as he slept.

The sun was just starting to slant between the part in the heavy blue drapes. The light glinted on the dark layer of whiskers covering his square jaw. She'd never noticed how thick and lush his eyelashes were before. Or that tiny scar just above his eyebrow.

Then again, she hadn't seen him in ten years. No doubt he had scars, both inside and out, that she didn't know anything about. She had scars, too, but at this moment they didn't seem to matter.

Gracie snuggled against his large, naked body, savoring the feel of his skin against her own. She closed her eyes as she remembered the delicious way he'd made love to her last night. More than anything, she wanted to repeat the experience.

But Gilbert was sleeping so deeply that she didn't want to disturb him. No doubt he was exhausted from his long flight from Boston—as well as the erotic trip they'd made together from friends to lovers last night.

It had been touch-and-go for a while. Gracie thought she'd had him when she'd stripped off her stockings, amazing even herself at her audacity. But he'd turned right around and started watching that videotape, seemingly oblivious to the fact that she'd been willing to strip off a lot more.

Fortunately that kiss had changed everything. She suppressed a shiver of delight, remembering all the places that he'd kissed her. Gilbert knew how to make love to a woman even better than he knew how to dance.

He was simply amazing.

But that wasn't the only word she could use to describe him. He was smart, sexy, funny. Her best friend. What more could a girl want?

That question caused her smile to fade. She did want more. But despite the incredible passion they'd shared, he hadn't said anything about staying past the weekend. This might just be a fling for him.

Hadn't she initially planned it that way herself?

She swallowed a sigh, realizing she'd never envisioned a night quite like the one they'd shared. The way he'd touched her. The way he'd held her. No man had ever made her feel so *cherished* before. That was the only word she could use to describe it.

And that's why she knew, deep down in her heart, that this couldn't just be another fling for him.

The melodic chirp of her cell phone made her sit up in bed. She glanced over at Gilbert, who was still fast asleep. Not wanting to wake him, she rose silently off the mattress and retrieved her purse off the chair. After digging inside, she plucked out her ringing cell phone, then carried it into the bathroom and closed the door.

She flipped open the phone, wondering who could possibly be calling her this early. "Hello?"

"Gracie, is that you?"

The deep voice sounded familiar, but she couldn't quite place it. "Yes, who is this?"

"It's Gilbert. I need your help."

"Try again." It was too early in the day for practical jokes. She leaned against the sink, the marble against her bare bottom a chilly reminder that she was naked. At the moment, she wanted nothing more than to climb back in bed with Gilbert and warm herself against his body.

"Gracie, what's wrong with you?"

"Nothing's wrong," she replied, losing her patience. "It's just that you're not Gilbert and it's too early to play games."

"Of course it's me," the man replied, an edge to his voice. "Gilbert Holloway, your best friend from high school."

His voice *did* sound eerily familiar, but she knew it was impossible. Time to call his bluff. "How can you be Gilbert when he's with me right now?"

"What?" The question was almost a shriek.

"You can't be Gilbert Holloway because he's here with me now. He's been with me all night."

"Oh, no." The man's groan carried over the line. "Oh, Gracie, I can't believe this is happening. Look, I'm Gilbert. I swear to you, I'm Gilbert."

She wondered if some of her old classmates had been up all night planning this prank. They'd probably seen her and Gilbert leave together and put two-and-two together. "I'm hanging up now."

"No! Wait. Please." The entreaty in his voice made her pause. This didn't sound like a joke. It sounded like a man desperate for her to believe him. *It sounded like Gilbert.*

She shook off that unsettling thought. This call had to be a joke. But how would any of her old classmates get her cell phone number? Gilbert had both her home number and her cell phone number, even though he'd always chosen to talk to her via e-mail. None of this made any sense.

"Who is this?" she demanded, hating that this man had ruined her morning. The guy on the line simply could not be Gilbert Holloway—he was in a bed just a few feet away from her.

Despite her words, she couldn't bring herself to hang up the phone. There was something about the caller—something about his voice—that kept her on the line.

"Look, I talked to someone who made it to the reunion," the caller said. "She told me there was a man there pretending to be me. I don't know what's going on, Gracie, but you have to believe me. I'm Gilbert."

"No," she breathed into the phone.

"I'm Gilbert Leopold Holloway," he said firmly. "I was named after my grandfather and lived in the same house where he was born at 1324 Mesquite

Road. That house was yellow with black shutters. You used to say it reminded you of a bumblebee."

An icy chill swept through Gracie that she couldn't blame on the cold marble. The voice sounded like Gilbert. And who else would know how she used to describe his old house? She passed it every day on her way to work. The new owner had repainted it years ago. Now it was white with pine-green shutters.

She closed her eyes, feeling a little dizzy. This couldn't be happening. The imposter story was ludicrous. Gilbert Holloway was right here with her. In bed. She opened her eyes, then peeked through the bathroom door just to see if he was the one playing the joke. But he was still asleep, no cell phone in sight. Besides, she reminded herself, he'd been asleep when it had rung.

She closed the bathroom door again, catching her reflection in the mirror. The color had drained from her face and her hair was a mess. Maybe this was a nightmare and she'd wake up soon. But the persistent crackle of the cell phone in her ear told her it was all too real.

"Where are you?" she asked him.

"I can't tell you. Not yet anyway."

"How do I know this is really Gilbert Holloway?" she insisted, still not wanting to believe it was true.

He hesitated for a moment, then said, "Do you remember when I asked you to the prom and you turned me down?"

"I didn't turn Gilbert down," she countered, not

ready to admit it was really him. "I just thought we'd have more fun away from all the hoopla."

"We went to that pizza parlor on Cummings Street. You started to order a pepperoni pizza, but I said we should live dangerously and order something else. Do you remember what it was?"

"Do you?" she challenged, hoping he'd be wrong.

"Canadian bacon and pineapple," he replied without missing a beat. "You loved it and I hated it. We had to pull over when I got sick on the way back to my house that night. Now do you believe me?"

Gracie sagged against the sink, barely resisting the impulse to hang up the phone and forget that this call had ever happened. But she couldn't go back now. She knew it was Gilbert on the line—which left her with another very important question.

"Then who is this man pretending to be you?" she choked out.

"I don't know," Gilbert replied, his voice frazzled. "There are a lot of people after me, Gracie. It could be any one of them. I'm in trouble. Big trouble."

Trouble didn't even begin to describe her situation. She'd slept with a stranger. Even worse, a liar. If the man would deceive her about his identity, even going as far as sleeping with her, what else would he do?

"Tell me what's going on, Gilbert?"

"I can't go into it now, Gracie. I don't have much time. But you need to get away from that man. I'll contact you again soon. Either later today or tomorrow. I need to get that tape back."

"Tape?" she echoed.

"The Burns and Allen tape I sent you a few days ago. Do you still have it?"

"Of course, I still have it. But I don't understand any of this."

"Look, I gotta go. Please, be careful. I'd hate myself if anything happened to you. Promise me, Gracie."

"I promise," she replied. "But—"

The phone went silent and she knew he wasn't on the line anymore. For a moment she just stood there, trying to absorb what had just happened.

Gilbert wasn't Gilbert.

The stranger in that bed had fooled her last night. Fooled everyone at the reunion. Gracie snapped the cell phone shut, furious with herself. She'd known it wasn't him the moment she'd seen him. But she'd let that name tag convince her, as well as her other classmates, who seemed to accept that he was Gilbert as readily as she had.

How could she have been so stupid?

How could she have slept with him?

A hot flush suffused her body when she thought of how eager she'd been to fall into his arms. So ready to believe that the handsome hunk in front of her was her geeky friend from high school. She'd been a much too willing victim of his deception.

Tears pricked her eyes when she thought of everything that had happened between them. He'd duped her so easily he must have laughed himself silly when she'd fallen asleep last night. But why would he make love to her?

That made no sense.

Unless he wanted the videotape, too. That possibility seemed like a certainty when she replayed their conversation from last night in her mind. They'd danced, talked. But he hadn't said a word about going up to his hotel room until she'd pulled the videotape out of her purse.

She remembered the strange way he'd acted when they'd first entered his room. Almost as if he was trying to avoid her. But she'd pushed ahead, blindsiding him with that kiss until he hadn't put up a fight anymore.

Humiliation washed over her. She'd made a complete fool of herself. Falling for the man's masquerade to the point of making love to him! That beautiful night—the night Gracie thought she'd remember the rest of her life—had been a complete sham.

All she wanted to do now was get as far away from him as possible. The only way this situation could get any worse was if she had to face him again.

Determined to disappear before that could happen, Gracie opened the bathroom door, wincing at the slight squeal of the hinges. The stranger still lay asleep in the bed, one arm stretched out over her pillow.

She swept up her clothes and hastily pulled them on, leaving half the buttons undone and her blouse untucked. Then she grabbed her purse and headed for the door. But as her hand touched the knob she remembered the videotape.

Swallowing a groan of frustration, she turned

around and headed back toward the television cabinet, keeping her gaze averted from the bed. She didn't want to look at the man again—didn't want to remember all the intimate things he'd done to her. All the things they'd done together.

She ejected the tape from the VCR, then stuffed it into her purse as she scrambled for the door. The creak of mattress springs sounded behind her, but she didn't hesitate as she bolted out of the door, letting it slam shut behind her.

Her dream of seducing Gilbert Holloway had turned into a nightmare. And something told her that nightmare was just the beginning.

ZACH AWOKE to the sound of a door slamming. He rubbed the sleep out of his eyes, then sat up, the sheet slipping down to his waist. For a moment, he couldn't place his surroundings. This wasn't his bed or his room.

Then he remembered his trip to Texas and the reunion. The Claremont Hotel and Gracie. It had been a night he'd never forget. He placed his hand on her side of the bed. The sheets were still warm from the heat of her body.

He was ready to warm them some more, remembering how she'd come apart in his arms last night. Hell, he'd barely held it together when he'd exploded inside of her. He wanted to do it again. Right now, in fact.

A good night's sleep had eased his guilt. There'd be plenty of time to reveal his identity. Better to do it slowly and earn her trust first. Then he could tell her the entire story, certain she'd understand the reasons he'd had to conceal so much from her.

"Gracie?" he called, assuming she was in the bathroom. He hoped she was still naked.

He swung his legs over the side of the bed and rose to his feet. He couldn't remember the last time he'd felt this relaxed. This…complete. Maybe Brannigan had been right about the vacation. But he knew it was more than the trip to Texas that had reinvigorated him.

It was Gracie.

He padded over the thick carpet to the bathroom, surprised to see the light on inside and the door standing half open. He pushed it open the rest of the way and stuck his head inside. No Gracie.

Perplexed, he turned around and scanned the hotel room. All her clothes were gone, along with her shoes and her purse. Zach walked to the hotel room door and opened it, peering out into the long hallway. But there was no sign of Gracie anywhere.

His gut told him something was seriously wrong. She didn't seem like the love 'em and leave 'em kind of girl. Not after what they'd shared last night.

In his mind, he went over every moment with her, trying to remember if he'd done something or said something to offend her.

But he was coming up blank. Unless…

Was it possible she'd figured out he wasn't Gilbert? Maybe sometime during the night Gracie had realized she'd made love to the wrong man. That thought made him feel sick inside. But he didn't know if it was true. There might be another reason she'd disappeared on him—like an emergency at the bookstore.

He walked over to the nightstand and pulled the telephone book from the drawer. After looking up the number for Between the Covers, he picked up the telephone receiver and dialed it, letting it ring ten times before he finally hung up.

Zach hated not knowing what was going on. Hated the sensation of being out of control of any situation. If something was wrong, then he wanted to help. Even if there was no dire reason for her sudden disappearance, he didn't want her running around Kendall alone—not after his conversation with Allison.

He took a deep breath and reined in his imagination. Now was not the time to panic. What he needed to do was shower and shave. Maybe a few minutes under a hot spray of water would clear his head. With any luck, Gracie had just gone out to get breakfast and would be waiting for him when he got out.

Bagels in bed sounded like the perfect way to start the day.

But when Zach stepped out of the bathroom twenty minutes later, the hotel room was still empty. He walked over to the bed and picked up her pillow, inhaling the scent of her perfume, which was still on the fabric. It hadn't been a dream. Gracie had been here with him last night, slept with him, made love with him.

So why had she run off without waking him?

Zach figured he had two choices. Forget about her or find out why she'd run out on him without even saying goodbye.

The choice was so easy to make it scared him.

6

ZACH DIDN'T START to panic until he turned his rental car onto the street where Gracie lived and saw a police cruiser sitting in front of it. Remembering Allison's veiled threat, he swerved to the curb, then jumped out of the car and ran up to the front porch.

If anything had happened to Gracie...

The battered front door stood open, hanging half off its hinges, and he could see the desolation inside. All her furniture was overturned in the living room, the ripped cushions spilling their white stuffing onto the beige carpet.

He stepped inside the house and glimpsed the broken dishes and pottery shards littering the kitchen linoleum. Books lay everywhere, the pages torn out and crumpled over the floor. Tiny shards of glass glittered in the rays of the morning sun that shone through a broken window.

A hurricane could have ripped through Kendall and caused less damage.

His years as a cop told Zach that this was more than a simple break-in. There was anger behind this crime. Maybe even hate.

His chest tightened as he scanned the room for blood, his mind flashing back to the day he'd found Ray bleeding on the floor at Holloway's house. The same sense of dread filled him now as he moved farther into the house, taking care not to disturb anything.

The sound of a gasp made him turn and he saw Gracie staring at him from the hallway. Her face paled and he could see her pulse jumping in her throat.

"What are you doing—?" she began.

Before she could get the words out, Zach crossed the short distance between them and swept her into his arms. "Thank God, you're all right."

Relief crashed through him, making it hard to breathe. He savored the feel of her in his arms, warm and soft and unharmed. If he'd had any doubt about his feelings for her before, he knew now that this was more than a long-distance infatuation. Last night had been his first clue. Today was his confirmation.

Gracie struggled in his embrace, her hands pushing hard against his chest. "Let go of me!"

He loosened his grasp, pulling away just far enough to take a quick inventory of her body and reassure himself she wasn't hurt.

"I said let me go!" she cried, twisting out from beneath his hands.

A cop emerged from another room and scowled at Zach, his hand reaching for his holster. "Back off. Now."

Zach released her immediately, aware that she

didn't share his warm, fuzzy feelings. Just the opposite, in fact. Anger blazed in her blue eyes, turning them almost sapphire. The high blush on her cheeks was almost the same color as the red tank top she wore.

Zach held up both hands to show the cop he didn't mean any harm. "It's okay. I'm a...friend."

"That's not true!" Gracie whirled around to face the cop. "This man pretended to be an old classmate of mine at my high school reunion last night. The truth is that I've never met him before. But he lied—about his name and his life. About everything."

The cop arched a brow in Zach's direction. "Is that so?"

"I can explain," Zach began, wishing he knew where to start. It was a long story and neither the cop nor Gracie looked like they were in the mood to hear it.

"Explain this," Gracie cried, motioning to the chaos surrounding them. "Was it your job to distract me so your accomplices could ransack my house?"

He stared at her. "You think I'm to blame for this mess?"

"What else am I supposed to think?" she replied, her voice rising. "You showed up at the reunion under false pretenses and played the part of Gilbert to perfection. That obviously took some planning."

"You're reading this all wrong," Zach told her. But he found himself reluctant to clarify it for her. Because in the light of day—and in the light of her anger—he saw himself through her eyes. It wasn't a flattering picture. He hadn't ransacked her house but he'd done something far worse.

"I'm sorry," he said, knowing it was too late for an apology. He'd manipulated her in the worst manner possible. It had been both thoughtless and selfish. He doubted she'd ever forgive him for it, no matter how noble his intentions.

She turned to the cop. "Are you going to arrest him or not?"

The cop looked between the two of them, then fished a notepad and pen out of his shirt pocket. "I'll need a few more details first," he looked up at Zach, "such as your name, sir."

Zach glanced at Gracie, hating that the truth had to come out this way. "Zachary Maddox."

"And how do you know Ms. Dawson?"

He hesitated. "We met last night."

"But it was all a lie," Gracie interjected. "He pretended to be Gilbert Holloway, an old friend of mine. He led me on and…"

"And?" the cop prodded, looking at her.

"And this is all just a big misunderstanding," Zach concluded. The cop didn't need to know about their night together. It had nothing to do with the break-in and would only embarrass Gracie.

But she didn't seem to realize he only had her best interests in mind.

"Misunderstanding?" she echoed, staring at him in disbelief. "That's how you describe what happened last night? A misunderstanding? Tell me, Mr. Maddox—if that is your real name—what exactly did I misunderstand? You introduced yourself as Gilbert Holloway to everyone at the reunion. You knew things about him—and me—that only Gilbert would know. You've obviously been planning this for a very long time. Now I want to know why."

"Perhaps we'd better take this downtown," the cop said, flipping his notepad shut. "We can run a check on Mr. Maddox, just to make sure he's clean."

"That's not necessary." Zach reluctantly pulled out his badge. It was the only way he could get rid of the cop and have a chance to talk to Gracie alone. "I'm with the Boston Police Department. You can call my chief, Thomas Brannigan, to verify. He'll vouch for me."

The cop studied the badge, then handed it back to Zach. "Looks legit to me."

Gracie looked shell-shocked. "You're a policeman?"

"A detective," he clarified. "I've been investigating a criminal case involving your friend Gilbert for the past six months."

She shook her head. "That's not possible. Gilbert would have told me."

Zach wondered if now was the time to tell her he'd been reading all her e-mails for the past three months. Instead he said, "There are a lot of things you don't know about Gilbert Holloway."

"Then why don't you tell me?" she challenged.

His gaze flicked to the cop, who seemed to be enjoying their exchange. "This isn't a good time."

The same passion that had flared between them

last night was in her eyes now, though stirred by anger rather than desire. Despite her animosity, he found himself aroused by her. He wished he could take her in his arms and turn all that energy into something much more pleasurable for both of them.

"I'm still waiting," Gracie said, making it clear that sex was the last thing on her mind.

He wasn't going to say a word. Not with the nosy cop standing between them, ready to spill their story to his fellow officers down at the station.

Gracie spun on her heel and disappeared down the hallway. He heard a door slam shut, the noise echoing throughout the house.

"That is one angry lady," the cop said, stuffing the notepad and pen back into his pocket. "So what are you really doing here, Detective Maddox? Texas isn't exactly your jurisdiction."

"I'm officially on vacation," he replied, aware he'd need the cooperation of the Kendall police if he wanted to pursue this case.

The cop arched a brow. "And unofficially?"

Zach met his gaze. "My partner was shot protecting Gilbert Holloway. So I'm not going to drop the case just because the desk jockeys in my department think it's time to move on. But I promise to stay out of your way if you'll stay out of mine."

The cop studied him for a moment, then gave a brisk nod. "It's hell when a fellow officer goes down. I'm Sergeant Bill Hayes. If you need any assistance, just give us a call."

"Thanks." Zach wished Gracie had been as understanding. But he only had himself to blame for her reaction. He just hoped she'd eventually cool down enough to listen to reason.

Twenty minutes later, Sergeant Hayes finished processing the scene and cleared out. He'd told Zach that the odds didn't look good for catching the perp or perps who had invaded Gracie's home.

Whoever had trashed her house hadn't left any fingerprints behind or other incriminating evidence, further proof to Zach that this had been more than a random break-in. Kendall was hardly a hot bed of crime. According to Sergeant Hayes, this was only the second break-and-enter he'd investigated in the past three years.

That convinced Zach it was connected to Holloway.

Gracie walked out onto the front porch. "What are you still doing here?"

Zach steeled himself for her hostility before turning around. "We need to talk."

"I don't want to talk to you," she said, bristling. "The only thing I want is for you to go away!"

Her words stung, but he didn't back down. Zach knew she'd probably hate him before it was over, but he didn't have a choice anymore. "Sorry to disappoint you, Gracie, but I'm not going anywhere."

GRACIE STARED at the stranger in front of her, feeling sick inside. She was still grappling with the fact that someone had invaded her home, her privacy. The last thing she needed was this imposter making 'things worse. It only reminded her of what a fool she'd been last night.

"Then I'll leave," she cried, turning away from him.

He stepped in front of her path. "Not until we settle this. You have to let me explain about Holloway… and about what happened last night."

The contrition in his voice made her hesitate, but she knew it was probably phony, just like everything else about him. She had no idea if Zach Maddox was a decent cop, but he was a hell of an actor.

"What about Gilbert?" she asked, purposely ignoring his reference to their night together.

He motioned to the house. "Why don't we go inside so you can sit down?"

She wanted to refuse but her knees still felt shaky and something told her this conversation wouldn't be a short one. Brushing past him, she walked into the house and took a seat on the battered sofa, drawing her legs up underneath her.

Zach sat down on the broken wing chair, an antique piece that had been upholstered in pink damask before a knife had ripped it to shreds. His hands smoothed over the damaged fabric, reminding her of the way they'd slid over her body last night. The memory set off a traitorous tingle deep inside of her.

"Well?" she prodded, hating the effect this man had on her. Despite his deception, there was something about him that still attracted her, something primal that she'd never experienced before. *And never would again*, she vowed to herself, at least not with him.

He met her gaze. "I'll start from the beginning—about six months ago, when we discovered Holloway was involved in an Internet fraud case."

She had no reason to believe him, not when he'd lied to her from the beginning. But she'd already agreed to hear him out. "What kind of fraud?"

"Credit card thefts, to be exact." Zach settled back against the chair, his obvious discomfort making her feel a little better.

"So you're calling Gilbert a thief?"

Instead of answering her question, he asked her one of his own. "Do you remember that cyber-consignment shop business Gilbert started about a year ago? He sent a mass e-mail about it to everyone in his address book, trying to drum up some customers. You were one of the names on the list."

Gracie nodded, remembering how Gilbert had always had one get-rich scheme after another, even back in high school. When they were juniors, he'd opened a savings deposit box at the Kendall State Bank to store all his riches. But all his inventions had ultimately failed, though she'd admired his creativity with the foot-massaging shoes and the talking trellis.

"That cyber-consignment store, as you call it, was legit," Gracie informed him. "Sort of like eBay, but on a much smaller level."

"We don't think Holloway initially intended to defraud people," Zach replied. "But we're not so sure about some of his vendors. We believe when customers bought items from certain vendors, with

Gilbert acting as the middleman, their credit card numbers were stolen."

She found it hard to concentrate while in the same room with Zach, especially when her feelings toward him were so conflicted. The man sitting across from her had lied to her and made love to her. One an act of intimacy, the other of betrayal.

Gracie took a deep breath, trying to maintain her equilibrium. "I don't understand."

"Say you wanted to sell this chair on Gilbert's consignment Web site." He patted the arm of the wing chair. "You'd list it, along with a price. When someone wanted to buy it, they'd send Gilbert their name, address and credit card number and he'd forward that information to you.

"Now, since you're a law-abiding citizen," Zach continued, "you'd handle the information for its intended purpose, then discard it. But we believe one or more of the sellers on his site made other, unlawful purchases with those credit card numbers or even sold them."

"So this is all about stolen credit cards?"

"That's part of it."

"But it's not Gilbert's fault if the people he does business with are crooks."

"We know that," Zach replied. "But he's the linchpin to solving this case. We set up a sting operation in his home, hoping to put it all together, but something happened…"

Gracie looked up as his voice trailed off. "What?"

Zach rose to his feet and began to pace across the

carpet. She couldn't help but watch the way his body moved, the way his clothes molded to the toned muscles she knew lay underneath.

"Gilbert must have tipped off one of the suspects to our investigation, because some thug showed up at the house while we had it under police protection. Things got out of control…"

She waited for him to finish, but his back was turned to her now and she could see the taut line in his broad shoulders. Apprehension fluttered inside of her and she found herself barely able to ask the question that hadn't occurred to her before.

"Was Gilbert…hurt?"

Zach turned around to face her. "No…we don't think so anyway. But my partner was hit. He took a bullet in the back. He almost didn't make it."

Gracie shook her head. "I can't believe Gilbert would ever be involved in something like this. It just isn't like him."

"No offense," Zach said, his voice hard, "but you haven't seen the guy for over a decade. You didn't even recognize the fact that I wasn't him last night."

His words brought all her shame and humiliation flooding back. Gracie stood up, her voice shaking. "Get out of my house."

"Look, I'm sorry," he said, obviously realizing his mistake.

"Not as sorry as I am."

He flinched, but she didn't care. Gracie had always gone out of her way to avoid hurting other people, but Zach was different. He was a cop. A man in a position of power. A man sworn to protect, not use and abuse.

That's why he'd slept with her last night. He'd used her to help him with his case. And that was the only reason he was here now.

He rifled a hand through his hair. "Look, I was wrong to keep my true identity from you last night. I'll admit that. But we're obviously dealing with people who are desperate to conceal their crime."

"What does this have to do with me?"

"Because they've escalated the situation by shooting a cop. Now they have even more incentive to shut Gilbert up—and anyone connected to him. You could be in danger."

"So that's the reason for your charade last night? To protect me? That's going a little above and beyond the call of duty, don't you think, Detective?"

Zach took a step toward her, then stopped. "You've got it all wrong."

"Really?" Gracie said. "So you just decided on a whim to crash a high school reunion a thousand miles away from home? Were you hoping to find Gilbert there? Or maybe you thought I was hiding him?"

He moved so close to her she could see the gold flecks in his dark brown eyes. "Understand this, Gracie. My showing up at the reunion last night had nothing to do with Gilbert Holloway and everything to do with you."

His tone more than his words made her skin prickle with awareness. He wasn't speaking to her as a cop now, but as a man.

"Yes, I lied to you last night," he admitted. "Hell, I've been lying to you longer than that. Holloway disappeared three months ago. Who do you think has been reading and replying to all your e-mails?"

"You?" she breathed, the floor shifting beneath her feet. "The past three months?"

"That's right."

Gracie closed her eyes, reeling from this latest revelation. It certainly explained the change she'd sensed in those e-mails, the intimacy. She'd never even considered a romantic relationship with Gilbert until the past couple of months. Because the Gilbert in those e-mails wasn't the Gilbert from her past.

"Just so you know," Zach said, his voice softer now. "Last night wasn't about Gilbert or about the case. It was about me. About my need to finally meet the woman who I can't seem to forget."

Despite everything, Gracie found herself wanting to believe him, wanting it so badly that it scared her. But she'd learned the hard way that this kind of longing meant disaster loomed ahead. All she had to do was look around at the chaos in her house—and her life—to realize it had already arrived.

Courtesy of Zach Maddox.

She walked to the door, turning to look one last time at the man she had thought was a dream come true, the man she'd thought was Gilbert. "I'm leaving now and I want you gone before I come back. Understood?"

She didn't wait for him to reply, walking out of the house before he could even open his mouth. Her head spun with everything he'd just told her and she needed time to sort it all out.

Time to bury another dream.

7

"I'LL TAKE ANOTHER cosmopolitan," Gracie said, pushing her empty glass across the bar.

Cat raised her eyebrows, but didn't say a word as she started mixing another drink. Most of the Monday lunch crowd had already left, but a few stragglers remained seated throughout the bar.

"So what's Laine doing out in California?" Gracie asked.

"Running away from her problems." Cat laid down a fresh napkin in front of Gracie, then set her drink on top of it. "It looks like you're gearing up for a little escape yourself without going anywhere. What's up, Gracie? You never drink at this time of day."

"There's a first time for everything," she muttered, taking a deep sip. "Like Saturday night, for instance, when I slept with a complete stranger."

Cat smiled. "So what's the problem?"

The fact that she wasn't horrified made Gracie feel a little better. Then again, Cat didn't horrify easily.

"It's a long story," Gracie replied, hating to burden Cat when everything was falling apart around them. Not only were they losing the bar and the bookstore, but she'd found out that Tess and Laine were both taking off for parts unknown. Things were already changing and she hated it.

"I love long stories." Cat pulled out a stool from behind the bar and sat down across from Gracie. "Besides, you've always been so cautious—with men, anyway. I can't wait to hear what drove you to do something so spontaneous."

Cautious. The word bounced around in her head. Is that how Cat and the rest of her friends saw her? Cat Sheehan never minced words. It was one of the things Gracie liked most about her. But the image the word "cautious" evoked wasn't exactly flattering.

"How am I cautious?" she challenged.

Cat rolled her eyes. "Please. You never date, even when you have the opportunity. And there have been plenty of Saturday nights in here when you've had the opportunity. The only man you ever talk about is Gilbert and he's a thousand miles away in Boston."

Though she'd borrowed shoes from Cat for the reunion on Saturday, she hadn't told her about her plans to seduce Gilbert. Trina was the only one who knew—and Paul—but she knew they'd never talk.

"I date," Gracie said in her own defense. "I'm just…selective."

"You've been playing it safe," Cat countered. "So I'm glad to hear you finally took a walk on the wild side."

"Not by choice. The night definitely didn't go as I had planned."

Cat looked at her. "That's what spontaneity means, Gracie. Something you don't plan ahead."

"I know the definition. But I wasn't trying to be spontaneous—I was trying to seduce Gilbert Holloway."

Understanding dawned on Cat's face. "So Mr. Perfect was in town?"

Gracie had never called him perfect, but thinking back, she had talked a lot about him to her friends. Maybe she'd even gone overboard in listing his good qualities. Now she wondered if she'd built him up in her mind with the subconscious purpose of making it impossible for any other man to live up to him.

Except Zach had. That thought came unbidden to her mind and she shook it away. Zach Maddox was nothing like Gilbert. She should know that better than anybody.

"Gracie?" Cat said, breaking her reverie.

She blinked, then struggled to remember Cat's question. "Sorry, I was...daydreaming."

Cat smiled. "So I see. And something tells me it wasn't about Gilbert. So who is this mystery man?"

She took a deep breath. "He showed up at the reunion pretending to be Gilbert. He fooled everyone. Including me."

Cat leaned closer. "Oooh, this sounds good. Was it some kind of Cyrano de Bergerac story where Gilbert was trying to woo you through another man?"

"Nothing so romantic," Gracie replied, though

she knew that wasn't quite true. That night in the hotel room had been the most romantic of her life—until she'd discovered it was all a lie.

Gracie drained her glass, then told Cat everything, including the fact that she'd spent the night in Zach's arms. The alcohol made it easier, though she still blushed when she admitted to seducing the man when he tried to tell her good night.

"Wow." Cat shook her head in amazement. "That is unbelievable. So what happens now?"

Gracie played with her empty glass, feeling hollow on the inside now that she'd spilled everything to Cat. "Nothing happens. Zach goes back to Boston, so I'll never have to see him again. And I go back to life as usual."

Life as usual.

No, that wasn't quite true. Her house was a mess. Her friends were leaving. Her dream to be a lawyer was over. And her bookstore was about to be demolished.

Her life couldn't possibly get any worse.

"What about Gilbert?" Cat asked. "It sounds like he's in a lot of trouble."

Gracie realized she'd been so concerned about her own problems that she'd spent little time considering what he must be going through. "When he called me yesterday morning, he told me he'd be in touch again soon. But I haven't heard from him."

Cat took the empty glass away from her, without asking if she wanted a refill. "Sounds like you'd better watch your back, especially after that break-in at your house."

"Gilbert would never hurt me."

"I'm not talking about Gilbert," she clarified. "I'm talking about the people that are after him. If they know you're his best friend, they might use you to get to him."

So maybe her life could get worse. She'd been so preoccupied with her plans to seduce Gilbert, then finding out that she'd slept with the wrong man that she hadn't even pondered the aftermath, despite that Zach had warned her of the same dark possibilities.

But if Gilbert needed her help, she'd be there for him—just as he'd been there for her these past ten years.

Zach was there for you, too.

Gracie pushed that unwelcome thought out of her head. Zach's masquerade might have fooled her for the past three months, but she wasn't going to be so gullible again.

She also wasn't going let what happened Saturday night keep her from getting involved with Gilbert's problems. The way Zach had talked before he'd left her house yesterday, he wasn't going to stop until he brought Gilbert into custody, with absolutely no mention of Gilbert's rights or what was best for him in this situation.

Another David-and-Goliath scenario. Only this time, Gracie wasn't going to let Goliath win.

Gracie fished the money she owed for lunch out

of her purse and set it on the bar. "Thanks for listening and for the cosmopolitans."

"Anytime," Cat replied. "Where are you going now?"

"I'm going to find Gilbert."

ZACH WALKED into Between the Covers, feeling as if he'd been there before. Gracie had described the place so many times in her e-mails that he could probably find his way around the store blindfolded.

The antique desk that had been in the Dawson family for three generations stood behind the counter near the entrance to the store. Rich oak paneling covered the walls, which stretched up to the twelve-foot ceiling.

Rows of towering bookshelves filled the store and he could glimpse a man seated in a small alcove. That had to be Paul Toscano, the writer she'd told him about who frequented the place on a daily basis. And the woman approaching him, wearing a sleeveless white shirt that revealed a tattoo of a phoenix on her upper arm, had to be none other than Trina Powers, her assistant manager.

"Welcome to Between the Covers," she said, smiling up at him. "Is there anything special I can help you find?"

"Actually, there is," he replied, his gaze still scanning the store. "I'm looking for Gracie Dawson."

"I don't expect her in today."

"Do you know where I can find her?"

Trina hesitated, sizing him up. "Probably. But I'm not sure I should. Who are you?"

The sound of a chair scraping against the wood floor echoed across the store and he looked over to see Paul emerging from his writer's nook.

"Need any help, Trina?" he called out.

"No, I've got it covered."

Seeing the expression on Trina's face, Zach realized that Paul wasn't the only one in the place with a protective streak—a fact he might be able to use to his advantage.

"My name is Zach Maddox and I'm a police detective."

She arched a skeptical brow. "I know everyone in Kendall and you don't work at the police department."

"I'm from Boston." He pulled out his badge, knowing she was the type of woman who would demand proof.

Trina took the badge from him and studied it closely before handing it back to him. "You're a long way from Boston, Detective Maddox."

"Please call me Zach."

"All right, Zach. Now why don't you tell me what's really going on?"

But before he could explain the door opened and Gracie herself walked inside. She stopped short when she saw Zach and for a moment he thought she was going to turn around and walk right back out again. Instead she squared her shoulders and approached him.

"Looks like I don't need to make introductions," Trina observed, glancing between the two of them.

Gracie didn't take her gaze off Zach as she spoke. "Will you please excuse us, Trina? I need to have a word with Detective Maddox in the back room."

"Of course," Trina said as Gracie turned on her heel and walked to the back of the store.

Zach followed her, his heart thudding in his chest. The heat of her anger enveloped him, just as her desire had in his hotel room. He'd accept her hate—accept any passion from her—since it was better than the alternative.

In his opinion, any emotion, even a negative one, was better than indifference. After his father had left, his mother had shut down her emotions, numbed herself to everything around her. Even him.

Zach had lived to make her smile—to evoke any reaction that showed she still cared. But those smiles had been few and far between. When she'd died five years ago, the emptiness inside of him had only grown.

Until Gracie.

He shook off thoughts of his past, telling himself to concentrate on the present. When they reached the backroom,

Gracie closed the door behind him, leaving them alone among the dusty stacks of boxes and old books. A lone lightbulb shone overhead, casting shadows over the room. The effect was oddly intimate.

He found himself wanting to tangle his hands in her silky brown hair and pull her to him for a kiss that wouldn't end until they were both naked on the concrete floor.

"Where's Gilbert?"

The question yanked him from his fantasy. He sucked in a deep breath and said, "That's what I was hoping you could tell me."

"If I knew, I wouldn't be here talking to you."

The fact that he deserved her anger didn't make it any easier to take. "Can we start over?"

"Why? So you can use me again to locate Gilbert? I'm not going to fall for it again, Detective. I want to find him so I can help *him*, not you. I wish I'd never met you."

"I know that," Zach said, hating like hell that she regretted their night together, a night he'd never forget. "But neither one of us can change what happened. The fact is that Gilbert is on the run from some very dangerous people. If you help me bring him in, I promise I'll do whatever I can to protect him."

Her gaze narrowed. "Why should I believe you?"

"Because I swear I'm telling you the truth." He knew his word would carry little weight with her, but it was all he had to offer.

Gracie stared at him, the moment stretching out so long that he didn't have a clue as to what she was thinking. "All right, I'll help you, Detective. Because I don't want anything to happen to Gilbert."

Zach chafed at the way she said the guy's name, remembering the way she'd called it out in his arms. But he was hardly in a position to complain. "Thank you."

"But just so it's clear," she continued, "I won't take orders from you. Understood?"

He gave a brisk nod, realizing he didn't have

much choice. If he wanted access to Gracie, it had to be on her terms. Even if that meant delivering Holloway to her. The man she'd wanted in the first place.

"What do you want to know?" she asked.

"Has Gilbert contacted you other than the e-mails and that videotape you received in the mail?"

Gracie hesitated, as if still not certain she could trust him. "He called me on my cell phone yesterday morning—at the hotel. That's how I knew you were an imposter."

Now Zach understood the reason she'd left the hotel so suddenly. Good old Gilbert had incredibly bad timing. "What did he say?"

"First, he had to convince me it was really him," Gracie replied. "When he found out there was someone impersonating him at the reunion, he got very nervous."

"I'm sure he did."

"I didn't understand what was going on," Gracie continued. "Gilbert promised to fill me in later, when I brought him the tape."

Zach's pulse picked up. "What?"

"The Burns & Allen tape. He wants me to bring it to him."

"When? Where?"

"He didn't say," Gracie responded. "He told me he'd contact me later to set up a meeting place."

There was no way Zach was going to let that happen. "You won't be meeting Gilbert or anyone else involved with this case. Just give me the tape and I'll handle it from here."

She shook her head. "I'm not taking orders from you, remember?"

Zach's duty to find Holloway battled with his fierce need to protect her. She was inextricably tied to this case in a way he didn't understand, a way that might put her in danger.

"Gilbert made contact with *me*," she reminded him, "and my house was ransacked. So I'm already involved."

She was right. But he didn't want Gracie in the middle of this mess. He'd already come close to losing a partner because of this case. He wasn't about to risk losing her.

"This could get dangerous," he told her. "I can arrange to have you placed somewhere safe, far away from Kendall until this is all over."

"Forget it," she replied. "I can't put my life on hold while you go on a wild goose chase. You know from reading my e-mails that I have to find a new location for Between the Covers in less than three weeks, plus manage the move and close up the old store. I don't have time to go anywhere—even if I wanted to."

It was clear to him that her loyalty to her dead aunt would prevent any of his arguments from swaying her. That left him with only one option. "Then let me protect you here in Kendall."

She took a step away from him. "No way."

"Just hear me out," he said, telling himself this was about the case and not about his feelings for her. "You want to find Gilbert—well, I can deliver him to you—with your help. We can accomplish more working together than we can separately."

He saw the uncertainty in her eyes and pushed even harder to convince her. "Let me stay with you— that way you can keep working at the bookstore while I monitor your house. Both bases will be covered in case Gilbert tries to contact you again. He's in big trouble, Gracie, and he knows it. That's why he's on the run."

Her brow crinkled. "Stay with me?" Then understanding flashed on her face. "You mean *live* with me?"

"I'll sleep on the sofa."

"Forget it."

"I'm not leaving you alone. Whenever you're at home or anywhere but work, I'm sticking with you." Zach needed to make it clear he wouldn't back down on this, even if meant she'd hate him for it. "It's either that or I contact the Kendall police and tell them to place you in protective custody. I think after what happened at your house, they'll accommodate me."

Anger flashed in her eyes. He wasn't giving her any real choice, but he still held his breath waiting for her answer.

"All right," she finally agreed. "I'll do anything to help Gilbert."

"I'll find him for you, Gracie," he promised, knowing he owed her that much. He'd let her seduce him, knowing she believed he was Holloway.

Now it was up to him to deliver the real thing.

8

SHE'D MADE A DEAL with the devil.

Only this particular devil had deep brown eyes and an unforgettable mouth that could melt away all her good sense. That had to be why she'd agreed to let Zach Maddox move in with her.

"You can sleep in Aunt Fran's room," she said, leading him down the hallway. "It might be a little frilly for your taste, but you won't be here long."

Better to set the boundaries now and let him know she considered this situation temporary. The sooner they found Gilbert, the sooner she could say goodbye to Zach Maddox forever.

"Look, I'll be happy to sleep on the sofa." He stood in the doorway of the second bedroom. "I don't want to intrude on you any more than necessary."

Too late. The last thing she wanted was to walk into her living room every morning to see Zach lying there, half undressed and disheveled from sleep. It would only remind her of their night together and she thought about that too much already.

"It's really no problem," she assured him.

All of her aunt's possessions were still in the room, since Gracie hadn't had the heart to sell them or put them in storage. Fran's complete collection of Harlequin Temptations were on an antique bookshelf next to her bed, their worn, creased spines evidence that she'd read them all numerous times.

Zach laid his suitcase atop the white chenille coverlet on the bed, then turned around to face her. "I'd like to take you out to dinner this evening, Gracie, if you're free."

The invitation surprised her. Then she realized he must be feeling guilty about lying to her. Good. She was in no mood to ease his conscience. "That's not necessary."

"I know it isn't necessary, it's just my way of thanking you for letting me stay here and assisting me on this case."

It was difficult to look into those brown eyes and remember he was the enemy. Okay, maybe not the enemy but certainly not her ally. Zach Maddox had shown her just how far he was willing to go to do his job. So she wasn't about to make it any easier for him.

"The only reason I'm doing this is for Gilbert," she replied, wanting to make that perfectly clear, "so you don't need to thank me. In fact, I'd appreciate it if we could just stay out of each other's way as much as possible while you're here."

"If that's the way you want it."

"It is. I'll be at the bookstore until late tonight." She turned toward the door. "Don't wait up for me."

Zach watched her walk out of the room, resisting the urge to go after her. She needed time to adjust to this situation and to the fact that he wasn't Gilbert. He needed time to figure out exactly how he was going to handle this relationship.

That wasn't his only problem. Brannigan would blow a gasket if he knew Zach was acting solo in going after Gilbert. But his boss was a thousand miles away in Boston. What Thomas Brannigan didn't know wouldn't hurt him or anyone else.

If he cracked this case, Zach was certain nobody would complain about it. Not when a fellow officer had been wounded in the line of duty. Besides, it wasn't costing the city of Boston anything for him to work the case during his vacation.

But what would it cost Zach?

He wanted Gracie—in his bed and possibly in his life. Hell, he might even be half in love with her. And now he'd promised to deliver Gilbert right to her door. The man she'd wanted all along.

What the hell had he been thinking?

Yes, he owed her. But she deserved more than a man like Holloway. And Zach could give it. The night they'd spent together wasn't just about sex. Zach had experienced enough one-night stands to know the difference.

He and Gracie shared a connection that was deeper than simple sexual chemistry. Yes, the attraction was still there and burning hotter than ever. But he didn't just want to go to bed with Gracie. He wanted to spend time with her, to learn everything about her. Even if sex wasn't part of the picture.

That was difficult for a man like Zach to admit. He had a powerful sex drive—one that had only increased since he'd met Gracie. But he'd be willing to put it on hold if it meant earning her trust again.

He'd almost blown it by deceiving her, but now he had one more chance. A chance to prove that *he* was the right man for her, not Gilbert Holloway.

Zach set his suitcase on the bed, then unzipped it and flipped open the lid. Despite the lavender and lace decor, the room had a cozy atmosphere that appealed to him. Maybe it was due to the fact that Gracie had told him so much about her aunt in those e-mails. Especially how much she admired Fran's strength and wit and gumption. All traits he could clearly see in Gracie herself.

Judging by all the framed photographs in the room, chronicling Gracie's life since she was a little girl, it was clear that Fran had loved and admired her niece just as much.

He removed a thick scrapbook from the top of the dresser, then stacked his clothes there. A fine layer of dust frosted the front cover of the album. Brushing it off with his palm, Zach saw the words Between the Covers inscribed in tarnished gold script.

Intrigued, he sat down on the end of the bed and opened the album. He found an old newspaper clipping taped to the first page and yellowed with age. Above the article was a photograph of two women standing in front of a brick building that looked familiar to him.

He scanned the short article, dated twenty-one

years ago, that announced the opening of two new businesses in that location, one a bar and the other a bookstore. His gaze moved to the caption beneath the photo, which identified the women as Fran Dawson and Brenda Sheehan.

He assumed that Brenda was the mother of Cat and Laine, since he knew they'd taken over the bar when their mother had remarried and moved to Toronto. Zach studied the photo of Brenda Sheehan, noting the determined set of her shoulders and the tilt of her chin.

His gaze moved to Gracie's aunt, surprised by how young she looked in the picture. Then he remembered that Fran Dawson had barely been fifty years old when she'd died, making her only in her late twenties when the picture had been taken. Close to Gracie's age now.

Fran had the same blue eyes as her niece, though she was several inches shorter. The same smile, too. Looking at her picture, so healthy and happy, he could understand Gracie's frustration with the insurance company that had caused her aunt so much stress. Gracie's desire to become a lawyer had been born from that experience.

Zach knew all about feeling powerless. He'd been unable to stop his father from leaving. Just like he'd been helpless to make his mother happy, no matter how hard he'd tried. That sense of helplessness was one of the reasons he'd become a cop. So he could stop some of the pain and misery and injustice in the world. So he could finally have a sense of control.

That was something he didn't have now, especially since Gracie had made it clear she wouldn't be taking orders from him. But he had no desire to control her, only protect her. He hoped she'd understand that in time.

Paging through the scrapbook, he found that it was a history of Between the Covers. The first dollar the bookstore had earned was in there, along with letters and autographed bookmarks from some of Fran's favorite Harlequin Temptation authors such as Jayne Ann Krentz, Carly Phillips and Jennifer Crusie.

There were pictures of book signings and book club meetings at the store, with Gracie appearing in most of them. As well as a book review column written by Fran for the local Kendall Tribune, until she'd become too ill to continue.

Zach sat there mesmerized, seeing a part of Gracie's life unfold before his eyes. Even after reading all of her e-mails, he'd never really understood why she didn't just sell the bookstore so she could go to law school.

All along he'd thought her connection to Between the Covers was the product of guilt. After all, Fran had taken her in as a teenager and raised her like her own daughter.

Now he realized he'd been wrong.

Gracie's connection to the bookstore was love. It was inexplicably entwined with her Aunt Fran—losing the bookstore would mean losing her aunt all over again. So despite that she hated working there, Zach knew Gracie would never let it go. Not without a fight.

He closed the scrapbook, realizing he was just the opposite. Nothing from his past mattered that much to him. His memories of his family were more about pain than love. Memories he'd rather forget.

The one memory he didn't want to forget was his night with Gracie. But he couldn't afford to dwell in the past or fantasize about the future, not when Gilbert was still on the loose and Gracie was at risk. Which meant he had to put his feelings for her on hold.

For now.

"YOU LET HIM MOVE in with you," Trina exclaimed after hearing the whole sordid story. "Are you crazy?"

"That would be a good word for it."

They both sat at one of the tables near the front door, watching the clock until closing time. Business had been slower than usual for a Monday night and the minutes had crawled by. Or maybe it just seemed that way to Gracie because she knew Zach was at her house, making himself comfortable. A fact that made her exceedingly uncomfortable.

She hadn't wanted to tell Trina about the high school reunion disaster, but Gracie couldn't have lied to her. Especially when Trina had asked to hear all about her night with Gilbert.

Trina shook her head. "So this guy lies to you, sleeps with you, then claims he wants to protect you. And you bought it?"

Her blunt assessment of the situation made Gracie bristle. "It's not that simple."

"Then explain it to me. Because the way I see it, this guy is just using you again."

A young man entered the store, giving Gracie a welcome reprieve from their conversation. She'd only given Trina the bare details of her encounter with Zach and their decision to team up to find Gilbert, not wanting to involve her any more than necessary. It was bad enough that she knew Gracie had seduced the wrong man.

As Trina walked over to assist the customer, Gracie returned to the inventory sheets on the table in front of her. The ones she'd been trying to ignore all evening.

According to her calculations, it would cost several thousand dollars to hire a moving company to haul all the store's books to a new site. *If* she could find a place in such a short time. She had some leads, but the few that were in her price range didn't have great locations.

Closing her eyes, she leaned her head back against the chair and indulged in a moment of wishful thinking. Instead of signing a new lease she could be signing up for her first year of law school classes. Her aunt Fran could still be alive, healthy and happy. And the man who had made love to her in the hotel could be the real thing, not an imposter.

Gracie opened her eyes and sighed. Reality sucked.

The truth was that night never should have happened. Law school wasn't in her future. Aunt Fran was gone forever. And now she was likely going to lose Cat, Laine and Tess, too. No doubt they'd all keep in touch for a while, but eventually they'd each drift off, pursuing their own lives.

Except Gilbert.

"Just a browser," Trina said, walking back to the table as the customer left the store. "Now where were we?"

"Talking about my recent insanity."

"That's right." Trina sat down across from the desk, adjusting her prosthesis at a more comfortable angle. "So this detective moved in, supposedly for your protection. My question is how do you know you're safe from *him*?"

"Because he hasn't made one move toward me since the reunion or one inappropriate comment about our night together." Gracie gave a small shrug. "It's not like I have much choice in the matter if I want to help Gilbert."

Trina's gaze narrowed on her. "Are you sure this is all about Gilbert? Because you sound different when you talk about this Maddox guy. You look different, too. So...alive. I know it sounds silly, but I can't think of any other way to describe it."

"That's ridiculous." But despite her words, Gracie could feel a warm blush creep into her cheeks.

The sound of a man clearing his throat made them both turn to see Paul standing near the door. He'd packed up for the day, the brown leather tote containing his laptop slung over his shoulder.

Trina glanced at the clock. "Leaving already? You've still got thirty seconds until we close."

"I'm having a few friends over tonight," Paul said, ignoring Trina's dig. "You're both welcome to come if you're free."

"Thanks, Paul," Gracie said, "but I'm planning to

check out a few rental opportunities I saw in the paper."

His gaze moved to Trina, who had been the real focus of his invitation. "The party should be a lot of fun. I'm having it catered by Hunan's. I know that's your favorite Chinese place."

"I've got to wax my legs," Trina said, rubbing one hand over her prosthesis. "But thanks anyway." Then she rose from her chair and walked to the back of the store.

Disappointment shone in his eyes as he watched her disappear between the stacks, and then he nodded toward Gracie. "I guess I'll see you tomorrow."

"Good night, Paul." When the door closed behind him, Gracie called out, "Okay, he's gone now. You can come out of hiding."

Trina emerged, carrying a book in her hand. "I wasn't hiding. I just need something to read tonight."

Gracie rolled her eyes. "Why sit home alone when you could go to Paul's party? It might be fun."

"I noticed you didn't accept his invitation."

"That's because I've got a new roommate, remember? He made it clear that he'll be tagging along whenever I'm not at home or here with you."

Trina grabbed her jacket off the hook, slipping it over her shoulders. "I can't wait to meet this guy. He sounds like a real piece of work."

But Gracie didn't want to talk about Zach anymore. She thought about him too much already. "I think you should give Paul a chance. He's a nice guy and it's obvious how much he likes you."

"Let's just drop it, Gracie, okay? I've got my reasons." Trina turned to leave, then stopped by the desk and picked up an envelope. "I forgot to give you this. It came in the mail today."

Gracie took it from her and immediately recognized Gilbert's handwriting on the front of the envelope. There was no return address. "Thanks."

She waited until Trina left to open it. Apprehension slid up her spine as she tore the back flap loose with her fingernail and pulled out the single sheet of paper inside.

Dear Gracie,
You're the only person I can trust right now. I know that sounds like something out of one of those old, corny thrillers we used to watch, but it's true. I don't know yet when I can see you. Things have gotten weird around here. In the meantime, please hide that tape I sent you until I can work something out.
I'm in big trouble, Gracie. Please don't let me down.

Love, G.

She read the letter again, hearing the desperation in each word. Gilbert was terrified. If only there was some way she could reassure him that help was on the way. Zach had promised to protect him—a promise she fully intended to make him keep.

But they had to find Gilbert first.

She turned the letter over in her hand, noticing the

small gray smudge on the back. When she rubbed her index finger over it, the gray substance adhered to her skin, fine and powdery. Her first clue to finding Gilbert.

And now she knew just where to look.

9

ZACH STOOD at the stove in Gracie's kitchen when he heard the front door open. He glanced at the clock, noting that she was later than he'd expected. Hardly surprising, since she'd been adamant about maintaining her independence during this investigation. A trait he admired about her—even if it did make him worry.

"Detective Maddox?" she called from the living room.

"I'm in here."

He didn't turn around, letting the anticipation of seeing her again buzz inside of him. He'd thought about her all day while digging up background information on Allison Webb and canvassing the Kendall area for any sign of Gilbert. Now she was home, safe and sound, and he could finally relax.

"What do you think you're doing?"

"Making us some dinner." He stirred the Spanish rice so it wouldn't stick to the bottom of the skillet. "I have chicken enchiladas in the oven and a pitcher of margaritas in the refrigerator. I hope you like Mexican food."

Gracie set her purse on the kitchen table. "Isn't it bad enough you have to invade my life? Do you have to take over my kitchen, too?"

Zach removed the skillet from the burner, then turned to face her. "I guess I didn't look at it that way. I used to fix dinner for my mom. She worked long days and was always too tired to cook."

His mother had never shown any gratitude for his efforts. She'd just sat down at the table and started eating. But at least she'd eaten, something that didn't happen if he didn't cook. So Zach knew she'd appreciated it without her having to tell him.

"Oh." Gracie looked contrite. "Sorry, I guess it's been a long day for me, too. Maybe I overreacted."

"No, I should have checked with you first."

He hated this stiff formality between them, especially after the very *informal* night they'd spent together. Part of him had hoped this dinner might dissolve some of the tension in the air.

"Look, I appreciate the thought, Detective Maddox, but this really isn't necessary. I can make my own dinner."

"This one is already made," he replied, pulling out a chair for her. "And don't you think it's time you called me Zach?"

She hesitated and he had to bite his tongue to keep from reminding her that they'd been intimate enough to be on a first-name basis.

"Fine," she relented at last. "Zach."

He smiled. "That's better. Now sit down and relax while I finish up here."

Gracie slid into the chair with a tired sigh. "It really does smell wonderful."

"And tastes even better." Zach pulled the enchiladas out of the oven, then dished up a plate for each of them. After he set them on the table, he poured her a margarita, then one for himself.

Gracie took a long sip, then set down her glass. "Almost as good as Cat's margaritas."

"That's quite a compliment," Zach said, seating himself in the chair opposite Gracie. "I'd like to meet her someday."

"Don't be so sure," she said, picking up her fork.

"Why not?"

She glanced up at him, a defiant tilt to her chin. "I'm afraid Cat doesn't have the best opinion of you, Zach. Not after I told her how we met."

He met her gaze. "I never wanted to hurt you, Gracie."

"Then you shouldn't have lied to me."

He winced at the pain he heard in her voice, knowing full well he was the cause of it. But he couldn't turn back time. All he could do was tell her the truth, no matter how it reflected on him.

"You're right," Zach said. "When I decided to come to Texas, I figured you'd realize I wasn't Gilbert the moment you saw me. I was going to come clean then, and just hope you'd give us a chance to get to know each other."

She looked skeptical. "Then why were you wearing Gilbert's name tag?"

He shook his head. "That's the crazy thing. Everybody there just assumed I was Gilbert without me even telling them. Then I got a break in the case." He set down his fork. "The first break in three long months. So I had a choice to make—continue the charade and the investigation, or tell you the truth."

"You couldn't do both?"

He shrugged, realizing he hadn't given her enough credit. "I didn't know how you'd react when I told you that I'd been reading all your e-mails to Gilbert. I thought you might be angry and give away my identity to everybody in that ballroom."

"Wait a minute," she said, her brow crinkling. "What break in the case are you talking about?"

"I met Allison Webb." He scooped up a forkful of rice. "She made it clear that she's been in contact with Gilbert and that she's somehow involved in all of this.

Gracie closed her eyes. "Oh, no."

He lowered his fork. "What?"

She opened her eyes and met his gaze. "Allison Webb was always Gilbert's weak spot. He was the smartest man I knew, except when it came to her."

"We all have our weak spots."

The way he said it made Gracie's stomach do a triple somersault, though she might have been reading more into his words than he'd meant. Had he really come to Texas just to meet her?

If she believed him, and part of her really wanted to, then his deception hadn't been planned. But it had clearly shown her his priorities. When the choice had come down to his case or her, he'd chosen his case.

Something she needed to remember. Especially when he kept doing things to lower her defenses, like making this wonderful dinner and looking at her in a way that made her itch to take her clothes off.

For one brief, insane moment she considered doing just that. Standing up and peeling off every piece of clothing, then straddling him where he sat. The thought made her squirm on her chair and she reached for her margarita, taking a long, deep drink.

"So tell me more about Allison," Zach said, oblivious to her thoughts. A good thing, too, since they were now living together and she needed to keep all those erotic fantasies to herself.

"I didn't know her all that well." Gracie set her glass back on the table. "Allison was different—a nonconformist. I think that's why she appealed to Gilbert. He always had a rebellious streak."

"So they dated?"

Gracie shook her head. "No. As I remember it, Allison barely even talked to him. He loved her from afar."

"Sounds like his taste in women was screwed up," Zach said. "Pining after Allison when he had you right by his side."

Now Gracie knew she wasn't imagining things. Zach Maddox was paying her a compliment. The only question was why? But instead of asking him, she decided it would be safer to change the subject.

"So did you cook for your mother a lot?" Gracie asked.

He shrugged. "She worked a couple of different

jobs while I was going to high school, so I always tried to have something on the stove for her. I liked trying out new recipes."

"Well, don't expect meals like this from me," she warned him. "Aunt Fran believed no woman should cook when there was take-out available."

He smiled. "I wish I could have met her."

Gracie suddenly realized this was becoming more like a date than protective custody. She couldn't let herself forget Zach's priorities. Or her own. "I received a letter from Gilbert today."

His smile faded. "Can I see it?"

She reached into her purse and pulled it out. "There's not much in it. But the postmark is local, so he must be somewhere in the area."

Zach took the letter from her, his brow furrowed in concentration as he scanned it. *"Hide the tape,"* he read aloud, then looked up at her. "What the hell is on that tape?"

She shrugged. "We watched it together in your hotel room. I didn't see anything unusual."

"Maybe we'd better watch it again," Zach said. "There might be something we're missing."

That was a definite possibility, since at the time she'd had nothing but seducing Zach on her mind. Gracie couldn't recall any details about the show, only details about Zach. Like the way his kiss had ignited a passion inside of her that she had never known existed. She'd done things that night, wonderful things, that she'd only read about, discovering how much better they were in real life.

The anger that had replaced that passion was burning away too fast, leaving her vulnerable to him again. She didn't want that to happen. But if her instincts were right, he wouldn't be around much longer.

"We don't need to watch the tape to find Gilbert," Gracie announced.

Zach looked surprised. "Why not?"

"Because I think I know where he's hiding."

THE NEXT MORNING, Zach rode in the passenger seat of Gracie's Miata, wondering why he didn't feel more excited at the prospect of tracking down Holloway. He'd been searching for the guy for the past three months, but there was a heaviness inside of him that he couldn't explain.

"How did you sleep last night?" Gracie asked, sunglasses hiding her beautiful blue eyes. Her window was half open, the wind blowing through her dark curls.

"Fine," he lied.

The truth was that he'd been up half the night tossing and turning, all too aware of Gracie sleeping close by in the next room. He tried to tell himself that if they hadn't already slept together, he wouldn't be suffering like this. But that was just another lie. He was more intrigued by Gracie than ever—sex or no sex—which blew his theory that coming to Texas would get her out of his system.

"How much farther?" he asked, telling himself to concentrate on the case. Her eagerness to find Gilbert dampened any hope that she might share his fantasies.

"About ten miles." Gracie rolled up her window, then switched on the air-conditioning. The Texas heat shimmered above the black top as they drove out of Kendall.

"The Holloways have owned this cabin for as long as I can remember," she continued. "It's very secluded. We'll have to park about a mile away and take one of the walking trails to the lake."

"Sounds like a good hiding place."

"It's the only place he could be," Gracie replied. "His parents moved to Florida several years ago and he doesn't have any other relatives around the area."

Zach knew if they found Gilbert there, he'd take him back to Boston before the day was over. Then Gracie would be out of danger. Once that was done, chances were depressingly good that he'd never see or talk to her again.

"I think I should go to the cabin alone," Gracie said, her words yanking him out of his lethargy.

"No way."

"Just hear me out." She glanced over at him, looking so incredible that she took his breath away. "Gilbert trusts me. He'll be more likely to open the door and let me inside if I'm alone. Then I can explain why you're here and that going back into custody is for his own good."

Zach didn't like the idea of Gracie alone with Gilbert—for more reasons than the issue of her safety. "I underestimated the danger of this case before and my partner almost died. I'm not going to make that same mistake again."

Gracie frowned. "How was his getting shot your fault?"

Zach sucked in a deep breath, guilt eating at him. He had no one but himself to blame for putting a rookie cop in charge of a situation that was more volatile than he'd ever imagined.

"My partner Ray and I were baby-sitting Holloway," he began. "It was a routine fraud case and we were assigned to gather more information for the assistant D.A. before she filed charges. Gilbert agreed to cooperate in exchange for immunity from prosecution."

Gracie turned the car onto a dirt road, the tires bouncing on the loose gravel. "But Gilbert didn't do anything wrong, did he?"

The trees along the road gradually began to thicken, soon blocking out the sun. "You have to understand how the police operate. Sometimes threats are necessary to achieve the desired outcome. We knew Gilbert was a dupe in the case, but he was involved up to his neck. If he had refused to cooperate, we could have made the charges stick."

She shook her head in disgust. "That is so typical. Pushing the little guy around until you get your way. What about his rights? Did he have a lawyer?"

"He never asked for one."

"And nobody suggested it might be a good idea, did they?"

"That's not my job."

She pulled off her sunglasses, setting them on the dash. "Of course not. That way the police have all the power. But it sounds pretty ruthless. No wonder he ran."

"He wasn't running from us," Zach clarified. "Whoever shot Ray was after Gilbert. A hired thug, most likely, who hadn't planned on bumping into the police. Ray panicked and pulled his gun. There was a struggle and the gun went off. If the neighbor hadn't heard the shot and called it in..."

"So how is that your fault?"

He turned to look at her. "I shouldn't have left Ray alone that night. He didn't have enough experience. Now he'll never walk again and I'll have to live with that for the rest of my life."

She kept her eyes on the road. "You can't change the past, Zach."

His throat tightened but he steeled himself against the emotions welling inside of him. "Maybe not. But I can keep from making the same mistake twice. That's why you're not going into that cabin alone."

A lake glimmered in the distance and Gracie pulled her car off the road, dry brush crunching under the tires as she slowed to a stop. "This is it. We'll have to go the rest of the way on foot."

He climbed out of the car, wondering if he should order her to stay here. But he knew it would be futile. She might not be a lawyer yet, but she had the instincts down pat.

Twigs snapped under their feet as they walked into the woods, the air around them fragrant with pine. Despite the narrow dirt path, Zach knew that if Gracie hadn't been in the lead, he would have ended up walking in circles.

"So did you and Gilbert come here often?" he asked.

"Only a few times," she replied. "He liked to fish and I liked any excuse to get away from the bookstore."

He was aware of her deadline for finding a new location for Between the Covers and knew that she was wasting precious time searching for Gilbert. That fact more than any other should have told him how important the guy was to her.

She stopped, a puzzled frown on her face as she looked around the path. "You know, I think I drove too far. Let's try going this way."

"Are you sure?" Zach said, as she veered off the path, deeper into the woods.

"No," she glanced at him over her shoulder, flashing a smile. "I guess you'll just have to trust me."

Zach found himself smiling back at her. "How can I be sure you're not going to ditch me here and go after Gilbert yourself?"

"I considered it," she replied and something told him that she wasn't joking now. "But I know you city boys can't handle the wilderness very well."

"I'm from south Boston. We're tough enough to handle anything."

Twenty minutes later, when Zach had almost given up hope, they walked into a clearing where a small cabin stood. All the paint had peeled off, leaving gray, weathered wood. Weeds surrounding the house, almost concealing the three crooked steps leading up to the porch.

"This is it," Gracie announced, turning to Zach. "The Holloway Hideaway."

Grime covered the windows and he saw a large hole ripped in the screen door. "Sure doesn't look to me like anyone has been living here."

"Oh, it's always looked like this. The Holloways liked the rustic charm."

In his opinion, it looked more rundown than rustic, but he had to admit the place would make a great hideout. He followed Gracie up to the front porch, then grasped her arm before she could knock on the door.

"Let me handle this," he said.

Gracie shook her head. "Gilbert won't run if he knows it's me. Just give me a chance to talk to him first."

Zach wanted to argue with her, but he knew she was right. He placed his hand on his shoulder holster, just in case.

After turning back to the door, Gracie knocked softly, then called, "Gilbert, it's me."

They both waited, but no reply came from inside the house.

"Try again," Zach prodded.

She knocked harder this time. "Gilbert? It's Gracie. Let me in." Then she moved over to a window and wiped the grime away before peering inside. The same grime Gracie had told him she'd found on the envelope sent by Gilbert.

"Is he there?"

"No, I think the place is empty."

Zach walked over to the door and tried the knob. To his surprise, it turned easily in his hand. "Looks like we can see for ourselves."

With Gracie behind him, Zach walked cautiously over the threshold. For a one-room cabin, it was much nicer on the inside than he'd expected.

There was an overstuffed plaid sofa and matching chair nestled around the fireplace. Colorful woven rugs on the hardwood floor. A small kitchenette with vintage appliances. The place was clean, if not modern. Clean enough to make him suspicious.

"Someone's been here recently," he said, swiping a fingertip over the top of the mantle. Then he showed it to Gracie. "No dust." He walked over to the waste basket. "And look at this."

She moved beside him, then bent down to pull out a fistful of empty candy wrappers. "These are Gilbert's favorite."

"I know," Zach said. "The guy's addicted."

"But we don't know how long they've been here."

He took one of the wrappers out of her hand. "You told me Gilbert hasn't been back to Texas for ten years."

"That's what I thought," she replied. "But as you said, it appears there's a lot about Gilbert that I don't know."

"Well, I do know that this particular flavor is new." He smoothed out the wrapper so she could read it.

"Watermelon-Kiwi?"

He nodded. "Gilbert preordered a case of it while we were set up at his house. That means he's been here recently."

She arched a brow. "You rely on a candy wrapper for evidence?"

He shrugged. "When you're a cop, you take what you can get."

Gracie turned slowly, studying the entire room. "So if he was here, where is he now?"

"Maybe he's just out for a while. We could wait."

She walked over to the kitchenette, opening the cupboards. "There's no food. I'd say he's cleared out already, if he was ever here to begin with."

"But where else would he go?"

Disappointment shone in her eyes. "I wish I knew."

Zach knew there had to be more clues here, but he just couldn't see them. All he could see was Gracie. She stood by the bed now and he wanted to lay her down on it and make love to her until nothing mattered anymore.

Not a smart move.

But he hadn't been feeling very smart lately. Better to leave before he gave into temptation. "Are you ready to go?"

She stood by the window, staring through the grimy glass. "Zach…"

The color drained from her cheeks as he moved toward her. "What's wrong?"

"I think there's somebody out there."

10

GRACIE STOOD looking out the cabin window, barely able to see through the layers of dirt coating the glass. But someone was moving out there. No, *two people.*

"Is it Gilbert?" Zach asked, reaching her side.

"No," she whispered, grabbing his arm as the images became clearer. "It's Allison and there's someone with her. But it's not Gilbert. I think it's a woman."

"Damn," Zach said, looking around the cabin. "I don't want Allison to see you here. She made it clear at the reunion that she resents the hell out of you."

"Why?"

"Who knows?" Zach looked under the bed. "No room there."

"They're getting closer," Gracie said, still watching them through the window. "It looks like they're arguing about something but I can't hear a thing."

He walked over to a small door and opened it, revealing a miniature pantry with shelves lining all three sides. "Think you can squeeze in here?"

She frowned at the tiny space. "Are you serious?"

"Completely." He glanced out the window. "We don't have much time."

Footsteps sounded on the porch steps and Gracie knew she didn't have a choice. She dove for the pantry, wedging herself inside. Zach edged in beside her, his large frame just fitting between the shelves.

It was so cramped they were barely able to get the door closed. Gracie tried to keep air space between her body and Zach's, but it proved impossible. Her back was pressed hard against the shelves, the edges cutting into her flesh. Her front pressed hard against Zach.

"Can you breathe?" she gasped, wondering how long they were going to have to hide in this small, pitch-black space. Even though the shelves were empty, it still smelled of cinnamon and cloves.

"Barely," he murmured and then his body tensed. "They're almost here."

Gracie could hear their voices now as the front door of the cabin opened, then closed again. "Are you sure we shouldn't confront them?" she whispered.

"Let's hear what they have to say first. We may learn something valuable."

She fought for breath, more a result of this intimate contact with Zach than lack of breathing space. She shifted slightly, finding a more comfortable position as the contours of their bodies fit more closely together.

Gracie swallowed hard, her heart racing in her chest. This little detour wasn't on the itinerary. But she couldn't do anything about it now—even if she wanted to.

"You've got some setup here, Allison," said an unfamiliar voice.

"Nice, isn't it?"

Even after all these years, Gracie recognized that faint Bronx accent in Allison's Texas drawl that had distinguished her from the rest of her classmates at Kendall High. Allison had hated Kendall and the "resident rednecks" as she called them, the moment her family had moved here from New York. A fact that she'd made plain to everyone she met.

Not exactly the way to win a popularity contest in high school, a place that had proved difficult for Gracie to fit in, too. The local students were big on football and tradition, resenting anyone who tried to make waves. And Allison loved making waves. She'd boycotted pep rallies and wrote scathing editorials in the school newspaper about the lack of culture and refinement in Kendall.

Gilbert had seen her actions as courageous, but Gracie had just thought she was a snob. That opinion had been confirmed the day Allison had laughed in Gilbert's face when he'd asked her for a date.

Now Allison was in his cabin, something that didn't make any sense to Gracie. When and why had Gilbert let that woman back into his life?

A cell phone rang and Allison said, "That's Gil. Come outside with me, Dorie. There's better reception."

Gracie heard them leave the cabin, their voices fading away. "Who's Dorie?"

"A cousin, I think," Zach replied. "I researched Allison's family at the library. There's a cousin named Doris Phillips who lives in Laredo. So it could be her."

"There's no way to find out in here," Gracie said, achingly aware of how good his body felt pressed against her own. "Now Gilbert's calling her and we can't hear a thing."

Zach hesitated, then said, "We've got to stay in here and hope they come back inside. If we go out now, we'll scare them off."

She knew he was right and nodded, bumping the top of her head against his chin. "Sorry," she whispered. "It's a little crowded in here."

"I noticed."

Gracie tried not to move, but her arms were trapped between their bodies and starting to grow numb. She wiggled a little, attempting to free them and heard a low moan emanate from Zach's throat.

"Please don't do that," he rasped.

"I can't help it. My arms are stuck."

He shifted slightly, the movement pressing her back into the shelves. Then he grasped both her wrists and brought them up around his shoulders. The change in position did give her more room. It also made her acutely aware of the intimacy of holding on to Zach in the dark.

"Better?" he breathed, his mouth so close she could feel his warm breath on her cheek.

Much better. "Yes, thank you."

"My pleasure."

She was so tired of fighting her attraction to him, so tired of just dreaming about what she wanted out of life. At this moment she wanted Zach and he was right here in front of her.

What was she waiting for?

Gracie knew she shouldn't move, but every nerve fiber in her body vibrated with the need to arch against him. To relieve the delicious pressure building between her thighs. She settled for sliding her hands around his neck and threading her fingers through the short, thick hair at the base of his scalp.

"Gracie," he said, his voice ragged. "This is... torture."

At least she wasn't the only one suffering. Neither of them could deny the sexual tension that had been sizzling between them since that night in the hotel room. She'd been fighting it ever since, but that just seemed to give it—and him—more power over her. Maybe it was time she took control.

"You're from south Boston, remember," she whispered against his ear. "Tough enough to handle anything."

Gracie remembered Cat's comment that she was too cautious and realized now that her friend had been right. Nothing like this had ever happened before and she found she was reveling in the excitement, the danger, the uncertainty. It heightened every feeling, including her desire for Zach.

She'd been numb for so long—putting her life on hold to care for Aunt Fran and run the bookstore. Zach made her come alive again. A prospect both terrifying and thrilling at the same time. But that was better than the inertia that had plagued her for so long.

Gracie brushed her cheek over his unshaven jaw

until he turned his head and caught her lips with his own. He moaned into her mouth and she held on as he kissed her with an intensity that touched her soul.

Zach slid his hands over her hips, pulling her so close she could feel the hard ridge of his arousal against the front of her blue jeans.

She stood up on her toes, bringing his hardness against the soft flesh between her thighs, the friction sending sparks of pleasure through her body. Gracie had never done anything like this before—never even imagined it. Now she couldn't imagine stopping. The fact that Allison and her companion could return to the cabin at any moment only added to the heated urgency of the moment.

Zach's hand slid over her hip, then around her thigh, until he was so close, but not quite touching the sweet spot between her legs. He held steady, silently asking her permission. She gave it by pushing against his hand.

Gracie closed her eyes as he began to move his fingers against her delicate flesh. Her head tipped back against a shelf as his fingers circled and pressed against the fabric of her jeans.

Heat spiraled inside of her, building into a flame that only his touch could extinguish. She writhed against him, wanting more, needing more, until the fabric beneath his fingers grew warm and moist.

"You're so beautiful," he whispered into the darkness, bringing his mouth down to nibble on her neck. Soft, tender kisses that heightened her desire for him.

The awkwardness of her position was soon lost to

her as he quickened the motion of his fingers, driving her higher and higher. She gripped his shoulders, hanging on as her breath came in quick, deep gasps.

"Now, sweetheart," he urged as her body tightened against him. "I've got you."

She barely heard him, losing track of time and space, unaware of anything except the magical movement of his fingers against her. Then she exploded, Zach catching her cries in his mouth with a long, deep kiss.

Her legs grew weak as the reverberations from her orgasm continued to wrack her body. A sweet, delicious ripple effect. Zach held her up, tenderly dropping kisses along her cheek and jaw until she could stand on her own once again.

Gracie was still trying to catch her breath when she heard voices inside the cabin once more. She had no idea how long they'd been there or when they'd come back in, aware that the solid wood door must have concealed the sound of her movements inside.

Zach held her in his arms as they eavesdropped on the conversation.

"So it's all set?" Dorie said.

"Only one more week," Allison replied. "Then I can kiss this Podunk town goodbye once and for all."

"Don't forget to hand over my share before you and Gilbert ride off into the sunset."

"That's up to Gilbert. He's still not too happy with the way you botched things up in Boston."

"That wasn't my fault!"

"You're the one who hired that cretin," Allison countered. "He was just supposed to cause a distraction so Gilbert could disappear, not barge in with guns blazing."

"Gilbert got away, didn't he?" Dorie said, her tone defensive.

"*After* that cop got shot. We still don't know if he's alive or dead."

Gracie didn't realize she was squeezing Zach's arms until his fingers gently loosened her grip. She couldn't believe what she was hearing. Allison made it sound as if Gilbert was to blame for everything. This had to be a ruse. Maybe she *did* know they were hiding in the closet.

"The cop's alive," Dorie replied. "I checked. He's in a wheelchair, but alive. So it's not like we'd be facing murder charges. And it's not like Gilbert hasn't screwed up, either. He's the one who sent that tape to the Dawson woman."

"He'll get the tape back," Allison assured her. "Don't worry about that. You just need to take care of everything on your end."

"No problem."

"Good. This thing should be wrapped up by the end of the week. If everything goes as planned, you'll get your share of the money."

Gracie heard the sound of footsteps and knew they were heading for the door. She resisted the urge to bolt after them and force Allison to admit she was lying about Gilbert's involvement.

The woman was setting him up. No doubt Gilbert was just as enamored with Allison as he'd been in high school, too blinded by his own obsession of her to see that she was trouble. Gracie knew she had to find a way to warn him before it was too late.

They waited several minutes before they finally emerged from the pantry. So much had happened since they'd taken refuge there that Gracie didn't know what to say.

Zach walked over to the window. "They're gone."

She straightened her clothes, noticing that Zach's shirt was half pulled out of his jeans. Then she saw the deep red finger marks on his arms. *Had she done all that?*

Her face warmed as she remembered exactly what he'd done to her. Something about that small, dark space had made her lose all control. Now she had to think rationally again, to put aside her feelings for Zach long enough to figure out what to do next.

He still stood at the window, his arms braced on the frame. "So what do we do now, Gracie?"

She wasn't sure if he was talking about their relationship or the case. So she answered his question with one of her own. "What do you want to do?"

He turned around, his gaze intent on her face. "I want to take you back home and make love to you. Hell, I want to do it right here."

She swallowed hard, but before she could reply, he continued.

"But we don't know if or when Allison is coming

back. The only thing we do know is that Gilbert is in this thing up to his neck."

Her warmth toward him chilled at the hard expression she saw on his face. "Don't tell me you believed her?"

"Didn't you?"

She shook her head. "Of course not. You said yourself that Gilbert was a dupe in this scheme. He was even helping the police."

"It doesn't look that way now."

"But you lived with him," Gracie replied, certain she could make him see reason. "You know he's not the kind of man to get mixed up in something like this."

"I've met all kinds of people who do all kinds of things for the craziest reason. Hell, look at us. I never imagined doing anything like what just happened in that closet." Zach moved toward her. "And I'm sure you feel the same." His words seemed to hold a double meaning.

She stared up at him, wondering if he was using her weakness for him to bolster his case against Gilbert. Just the fact that the thought had occurred to her proved that some part of her still didn't trust him.

Maybe it was her cautious nature taking hold again, but Gracie wasn't going to gamble with Gilbert's life or her own happiness to fulfill her sexual fantasies, no matter how tempting the prospect.

"We have a problem," she said, steering the subject back to safe territory. "You think Gilbert's guilty and I know he's innocent."

Disappointment flared in his eyes. "That's all you have to say? About this?" His gaze flicked to the closet, then back again. "About us."

"Yes." She turned toward the cabin door, not trusting herself enough to look at him, certain she'd falter under the vulnerability she saw in his dark eyes.

"Gracie, wait…" Zach moved beside her. "You're not going out there alone. In fact, after hearing what Allison had to say, you're not going anywhere alone."

"So you're going to help me prove him innocent?"

"No," he bit out, closing the cabin door behind him. "I'm going to prove once and for all that you've given your trust to the wrong man."

11

THE NEXT DAY, Zach was fighting the urge to hit someone, preferably Gilbert Holloway. Instead he settled for splitting wood in Gracie's back yard. It was hard work, normally hired out to the teenager next door, according to Gracie.

But Zach needed to relieve the tension that had been building inside of him since their interlude in the closet. He just wished the blisters on his hand would take his mind off the ache in other parts of his body.

Because she'd chosen Gilbert.

After coming apart in his arms, after hearing Allison name Holloway as the mastermind in the whole scheme, Gracie still preferred to give her loyalty—and her love—to a man who didn't deserve her.

Maybe Zach didn't deserve her, either. He picked up the ax and swung it over his head, bringing it down hard against the end of the log. A satisfying crack sounded as the wood split into two pieces. He tossed them onto the pile, then reached for another log.

The hot June sun beat down on him and he could

feel the beginning of a burn across his back and shoulders. He'd taken off his damp shirt an hour ago. Probably not a good idea to expose his Boston skin to these merciless Texas rays, but he'd been too hot to care.

The worst of it was that only a few steps away lay an air-conditioned house and a nice, ice-cold beer in the refrigerator.

Both tempting, but not as tempting as Gracie. She was in there, too, watching that Burns & Allen tape over and over again, looking for some clue that would lead her to Holloway.

Zach wiped the perspiration off his brow with his forearm, then attacked the next log. He needed to find some way to convince her that Gilbert wasn't the man she remembered. Words obviously didn't work—he'd been arguing his point since they'd left the cabin yesterday.

Which left him with one other option.

Despite her loyalty to Gilbert, even Gracie couldn't deny the physical connection between them. If he could make love to her again, break down her defenses until she was willing to listen to reason...

Zach split the last log, tossing the pieces onto the pile. Then he wedged the ax into a tree stump, his muscles throbbing in his arms. He'd be sore tonight. Hopefully, sore enough to drop into deep, dreamless sleep as soon as his head hit the pillow.

He sure as hell didn't want to spend another night awake and alone, not when he could smell the delicate scent of her perfume in every room of the house. It drove him crazy. Almost as crazy as the sight of her freshly laundered lingerie hanging from the shower rod in the bathroom. If he didn't know better, he'd think she was purposely trying to unravel him.

Wiping his damp hands on his jeans, he moved toward the house, ready to drown himself in a cold beer. He'd follow that with a long, cold shower—once Gracie removed her underwear from the rod.

He opened the back door, the hinges squeaking, then walked into the kitchen. The cool air hit him as soon as he stepped inside, a welcome relief from the heat. He just stood there, too hot to move, until he saw the note stuck to the refrigerator door.

Tossing his shirt over his shoulder, Zach headed for the refrigerator until he was close enough to read it.

Had to run into work. Be back in time for supper.

Gracie

Short. Impersonal. And directly against his orders. He swore under his breath as he yanked the refrigerator door opened and pulled out a frosty beer bottle. He'd made it clear to Gracie that she wasn't to go anywhere alone.

After twisting off the cap, he took a long swig, the icy amber brew washing down his parched throat. The way he saw it, he had two choices. Go after her or go take that cold shower. In the mood he was in, Zach knew going after her wasn't a good idea.

So after he finished his beer, he headed for the shower. If Gracie was lucky, he'd be in a much better mood by the time she got home.

IF ZACH WAS LUCKY, she'd be in a much better mood by the time she got home. At the moment, she was frustrated that he was too stubborn to listen to reason. She'd talked herself blue in the face since leaving the cabin yesterday, trying to convince him that Gilbert was one of the victims in this case. A victim who was about to be framed if Allison Webb had her way.

But Zach wouldn't listen to her. He was too caught up in his Tarzan routine to be rational. She'd left him chopping enough wood to last her for three Texas winters, all the while demanding that he know her every move so he could protect her.

"Right," she muttered to herself as she shelved the latest batch of book releases. "The only man I need protection from is him."

Trina popped her head around the corner of the bookcase. "That's the third time today I've heard you talking to yourself. Don't you know that's one of the first signs of insanity?"

"Then I'm a lost cause," Gracie replied, "because talking to Zach Maddox *is* like talking to myself. He's the most frustrating, bullheaded man I've ever met."

Trina grinned. "And that sounds like the first sign of a woman in love."

"Only if I really am crazy."

"Okay, so maybe you're only in lust."

Gracie sighed. "I hate to admit it, but that is a definite possibility."

"And the problem is...?"

"I already told you," Gracie replied, wiping a layer of dust off the shelf in front of her. "He's frustrating, bullheaded, bossy—"

"All unimportant traits when he's naked."

That was the real problem. It had been too long since she'd seen him naked. Four days to be exact. That time in the cabin didn't count since he'd had his clothes on. So had she, for that matter, which only made it more amazing that he'd been able to make her lose all control.

No man had ever done anything like that to her while she was fully dressed. So he did have *some* redeeming qualities. Most of them fully visible when he was naked.

"Naked just confuses things," Gracie said.

"Exactly my point." Trina pulled out one of the books that Gracie had shelved upside down and turned it over before sliding it back into place. "You claim he's bullheaded. I'm assuming that means he won't listen to your point of view."

"You guessed it."

"Then maybe you need a little naked *confusion*."

Gracie stared at her in surprise. "You mean sex?"

Trina nodded. "It is the oldest method of persuasion in the history of mankind. Or should I say, womankind."

"You think my having sex with Zach will solve all our problems?"

Her smile widened. "Even if it doesn't, you'll have fun trying."

The prospect was more appealing than Gracie wanted to admit. Part of her frustration with Zach stemmed from her attraction to him. Even when he drove her crazy, she wanted to ravish him.

"I can't talk about this anymore," Gracie said, feeling even more flustered than when she'd left the house. One look at him chopping wood, half naked and muscles bulging, had driven her straight out the door.

"All right, let's talk about the bookstore. I've got a good lead on a new location."

Gracie brushed the dust off her hands, then headed to the front counter. "Tell me about it."

"Remember that realtor who contacted us when the highway deal went through?"

"Barely. That was months ago."

"I know. But he must have kept tabs on us and heard the Kendall Historical Society rejected the building. Apparently, he's been calling all over town looking for empty spaces for us to lease."

"Why would he do something like that on his own?"

Trina shrugged. "I suppose he wants the commission. Face it, Gracie, we're not getting anywhere trying to find a place on our own. Time is running out."

Trina had a point. Gracie had been too distracted by Zach and too worried about Gilbert to give all her attention to the bookstore. If she didn't find a new place for Between the Covers soon, she'd have to pay double the moving costs—once to haul the books in storage and again when she leased a new space.

"Here it is," Trina said when they reached the desk. She handed Gracie a sheet of notebook paper with the address scribbled on it.

"Parvey Road?" Gracie read aloud. "Where's that?"

"On the other side of town," Trina replied. "The real estate guy said it's a new development that's looking for tenants, so it's in our price range."

Gracie tucked the paper into her purse. "I'll head out there now and take a look. Do you want to come along? Paul can watch the store."

Paul often stood in for them for an hour or two when Gracie and Trina both had to be away from the bookstore at the same time.

"No, I'm expecting a call from one of the girls in my support group. She's having a rough time, so I'd better be here."

"Okay." Gracie knew how important Trina's volunteer work was to her. She ran a support group for people who found themselves suddenly disabled, either through an accident or a medical condition.

Gracie headed for the door. "Wish me luck."

"Good luck," Trina said. "I'll slip over to Temptation and buy a bottle of champagne—just in case we get lucky."

Gracie walked out the door, relishing her freedom. Zach had been like her shadow these past few days, never letting her out of his sight. But even on her own, she couldn't seem to stop thinking about him.

Or about the old-fashioned method of persuasion that Trina had put into her head.

ZACH WALKED into the bookstore refreshed from his cold shower and ready to lay down some ground rules. Gracie might not be ready to admit that Gilbert was guilty of his crimes, but she needed to know that helping him could put her in legal jeopardy. A risk Zach wasn't about to let her take.

"Hello, may I help you?"

He looked up to see Paul Toscano standing behind the counter. "I hope so. I'm looking for Gracie."

Paul smiled. "Sounds like you have a hard time keeping track of her. I was here the last time you were looking for her."

"That's right. My name's Zach Maddox. And you're Paul, aren't you? Gracie's told me about you."

"Really?" His expression grew guarded. "What did she say?"

"Don't worry, it was all good. She told me you're a writer. And that you're very talented."

Paul shook his head. "My only talent seems to be handling rejection well," he replied, "in my writing and my life."

"Sorry to hear it. Maybe that will change soon."

"Oh, I'm sure it will," Paul said cryptically, "one way or the other."

According to Gracie's e-mails, the guy had it bad for Trina Powers, the bookstore's assistant manager.

Zach had thought it amusing at the time. Now that he found himself agonizing over a woman, he could definitely sympathize.

Unfortunately, he didn't have the time or the patience to play Dr. Phil. "Do you have any idea where I can find Gracie?"

"Not a clue. All I know is that she left here about half an hour ago."

Zach bit back an oath, wondering how he was supposed to protect her when she kept disappearing. "What about Trina? Would she know where to find her?"

Paul shrugged. "She got called away, too. That's why I'm working desk duty. I'm sure one of them will be back soon."

Zach reached for his cell phone on his belt, but found the clip empty. "Damn."

"Something wrong?"

"I forgot my cell phone."

Paul pointed to the desk behind him. "It looks like Gracie forgot hers, too. So lending you my phone probably wouldn't do you much good."

He was right. But that didn't make Zach feel any better. Not only was Gracie out there alone, but she didn't even have a way to contact him if she got into trouble.

Zach knew the odds of that happening were slim, but he didn't want to take any chances. Not with Gracie. He just wished she didn't have the power to distract him so much—like making him forget his cell phone. Zach never did things like that back in Boston.

He was spending so much time focused on Gracie that he hadn't been thinking straight.

Lust could do that to a man. But Zach knew that it was more than lust. Living with Gracie these past few days had shown him what was missing in his life. Someone to cook for and talk to and worry about. A real relationship.

A real home.

Paul cleared his throat, breaking Zach's reverie. "Do you mind if I ask your opinion about something?"

"Go ahead."

He pulled a small black velvet box out of his shirt pocket, then flipped open the lid to reveal an emerald and diamond ring. "What do you think?"

"Nice," Zach replied. "What's the occasion?"

"I'm going to ask the woman I love to marry me."

Zach wondered if he'd missed something in one of Gracie's e-mails. "Are you talking about Trina?"

Paul nodded. "You've met her. She's an incredible woman, isn't she?"

It was the kind of question that didn't require an answer. "I didn't realize you two had started dating."

"We haven't," Paul replied. "But we've been seeing each other every day for over three years. That's got to count for something."

It looked like he got to play Dr. Phil after all. Zach just wished he knew what to say. "Sure, but do you know if she feels the same about you?"

Paul shrugged. "All I know is that she thinks that prosthesis she wears will keep any man from falling in love with her. I thought if I proposed, she'd realize that I was really serious about her."

"A form of shock therapy?"

Paul grinned. "Exactly."

"What if she turns you down?"

"What have I got to lose?" Paul caressed the ring with the tip of his index finger. "I love Trina more than anything and this is the best way I know how to show it. If she turns me down, at least I gave it my best shot."

Zach stared at him, certain a stinging rejection was in the man's future. But Paul didn't seem to care. No, he did care, he was just willing to risk it, willing to put his heart on the line for the woman he loved.

A risk Zach hadn't taken yet.

"I've got it all planned out," Paul said. "I know Trina's working tonight, so I'm having a gourmet dinner delivered here right before closing time. I've got a bottle of Cristal cuvée chilling in the mini-fridge in the backroom. When the time is right, I'm going to pop the question."

"Well...good luck," Zach said.

"Thanks. I'm scared shitless. But better to feel scared than nothing, right?"

The words hit him like a sledgehammer to the gut. Without realizing it, Paul was the one who had taken on the role of Dr. Phil, making Zach realize what was really holding him back from admitting his feelings to Gracie.

He'd grown up with a mother who had numbed herself to relationships and to the world, forming a protective shell forged from too many broken dreams. A shell he'd never managed to break through.

What he hadn't figured out until now was that he'd followed her example. Zach had always pushed people away, using the excuse that his line of work had the potential for too much heartache. But the truth was he'd been trying to protect his own heart.

Now he knew that simply wasn't possible. He'd thought he'd been playing it smart when all he was really doing was playing it safe.

But no more. Starting tonight, he was going to engage in a form of shock therapy himself.

12

THE CLOSER Gracie drove to Parvey Road, the more she wondered if the real estate agent was playing some kind of practical joke on her. The neighborhood grew more dilapidated with each turn. A view of rundown and abandoned buildings, surrounded by trash, wasn't exactly the atmosphere she wanted for Between the Covers.

It was almost dusk, making it difficult to read the addresses along the street. The area was more industrial than retail, but the agent had said the neighborhood was undergoing revitalization. Maybe the trash lining the gutters meant they were still in the demolition stage.

The paved road led to a dead end, where Gracie saw a warehouse made of gray steel siding with an address that matched the one Trina had given her.

She pulled into the empty lot and parked near the door, keeping the engine running as she debated whether to go inside. There was no way she'd ever move Aunt Fran's bookstore to a place like this, no matter how desperate she was.

Then she saw a shadow move behind the glass

door of the warehouse. Startled, she shifted her car into reverse, ready to peel out of the parking lot. But the door opened and a man stepped outside.

It was Gilbert.

She cut the engine, then opened the car door, surprised to find her knees shaking. Despite his claims of weight loss and Lasik surgery, Gilbert looked much the same as she remembered him.

He still had shaggy dark hair that hung too low on his brow, Coke-bottle bottom glasses and a stout frame. Had he posed as the real estate agent and made the call to bring her here? Or was there someone else, besides Allison and Dorie, in on this scheme?

Despite her confusion, she didn't hesitate to enter the warehouse. She knew she had nothing to fear from Gilbert.

He held the door open for her, then followed her inside. Without saying a word, he enveloped her in a big bear hug. His clothing stank of stale sweat and she could feel the rough graze of his whiskers against her cheek.

"I'm so glad you came," Gilbert said.

"Why all the secrecy?" she asked, taking a step back for a better look at him. She would have recognized him anywhere, making her wonder once again how she could have ever believed Zach was Gilbert.

"Sorry about that," he replied. "I just can't be too careful these days."

"Gilbert, what's going on?" she asked, looking around the dank, empty building. There were water stains on the ceiling and insulation jutting from holes in the wall.

"It's a long story," he replied, steering her toward a small vinyl card table and two chairs, all scarred with wear and splashed with different colors of paint. "How much time do you have?"

"Time enough for you to tell me you had nothing to do with the Internet fraud—or that cop's shooting."

"Cripes," Gilbert said, staring at her in amazement. "How much do you know?"

So she told him everything—from Zach's appearance at the reunion to the break-in at her house to overhearing the conversation at the cabin between Allison and Dorie. The only thing she left out was her night with Zach and the fact that she was living with him now.

Gilbert kept shaking his head as she relayed her story, reinforcing her belief that he truly was innocent of all the charges Zach had laid at his feet.

"I can't believe this is happening to me." His face grew mottled and panic shone in his eyes. "What the hell am I going to do now?"

"Let me help you," Gracie entreated. "We'll go to Zach and you can tell him your story. Between the two of us we convince him that you're not to blame for any of it."

Gracie wished she could be as confident as she sounded. Zach hadn't listened to her yet. But she had to try. She couldn't leave Gilbert alone in a place like this.

"That's the problem, Gracie." Gilbert stood up and began to pace in front of her. "I *am* to blame."

Disappointment welled in her throat, but she still couldn't believe her best friend from high school would hurt anyone. He'd even refrained from killing spiders whenever they'd cleaned out the cabin every spring, preferring to catch them in a glass and release them outside.

"Tell me what happened," she said softly, "from the beginning."

He took a deep breath. "It all started when I sent out those mass e-mails about my Internet consignment store. You got one, didn't you?"

She nodded. "I even tried to buy some rare books you had on sale there, but someone outbid me."

"That was me," he admitted. "By that time, I'd figured out what was happening with the credit card thefts and I didn't want you involved."

"If you knew, why didn't you go to the police right away?"

"Because of Allison."

His voice softened when he said her name and Gracie recognized the same glazed look he'd had in his eyes back in high school whenever Allison Webb had walked by. What she couldn't figure out was how the woman could still have this effect on him after ten years.

Then she thought about Zach and knew a hundred years could pass and she'd still feel the same sizzle when he walked into the room, as well as the same spiritual connection.

But Gracie hoped she'd never compromise her values because of him. Or worse, betray the people around her. Gilbert had done both.

"Look, I know you don't understand." Gilbert knelt in front of her chair. "But you've got to believe me. I never wanted anyone to be hurt."

She didn't know what to believe anymore. "What am I doing here?"

"I need you to do one favor for me," he entreated. "Then I'll never ask you for anything again."

Apprehension skittered up her spine. "What?"

"Bring the videotape to me tomorrow night. Same time. Same place."

She rose to her feet. "What does that videotape have to do with any of this? I've watched it over and over again. There's nothing on it but a bunch of old comedy routines."

"It's better if you don't know." Gilbert used the table for leverage to pull himself off the floor. "Just bring me the tape, then this entire mess will be over."

"How?"

He hesitated. "I've got the information the police want, but I need to be the one to give it to them. I sent the tape to you for safekeeping while I was on the run."

"Let's go to them now," Gracie suggested. "I'll drive and we can pick up the tape at my house on the way. You know I'll vouch for you."

He shook his head. "Not without Allison. She has to be there, too."

"Gilbert…"

"No," he interjected. "I mean it. I won't turn my back on her now."

Gracie rubbed her hands over her arms, chilled by the dank air and by Gilbert's blind devotion to a woman who didn't deserve him. "Where is Allison?"

"I can't tell you."

She blinked. Gilbert had always told her everything. "Why not?"

"Because I promised not to tell anyone. I'm sorry, Gracie, but I gave her my word."

"Then give me your word, too," she said, taking a deep breath. "If I bring you the tape, promise me that you'll go to the police right away."

"I promise," he said without hesitation.

She looked around the warehouse, hating the thought of leaving him here. "Do you need anything, Gilbert? Food? Some blankets?"

He shook his head. "I'm not staying here. Don't worry, I'll be fine." Then he glanced at his watch. "Time to say good night, Gracie."

Her throat tightened. He sounded so much like the old Gilbert and looked like him, too. But he'd changed and so had she. The man she'd built up in her dreams, comparing him to every other man she'd ever met, had never really existed.

Gracie walked to the door, sensing that there was still something that Gilbert wasn't telling her. But she didn't want to linger in this creepy place any longer than necessary.

Especially when she only had twenty-four hours to decide whether to tell Zach that she'd found his prey.

GRACIE ARRIVED HOME that night to find the house dark and empty. She flipped on a light in the living room, surprised that Zach wasn't there waiting to rip into her for leaving without telling him.

A twinge of apprehension rippled through her. She walked down the hallway and opened the door to her aunt's old room. The bed was neatly made and she didn't see his suitcase anywhere.

Zach had left her.

No goodbye speech, not even a note. Disappointment thickened in her throat and she felt a ridiculous urge to cry. He'd driven her crazy these past few days, but now that he was gone there was an emptiness inside of Gracie that threatened to overwhelm her.

The Burns & Allen videotape still sat on top of the television set. He hadn't taken it with him. Maybe he'd already gotten a tip on where to find Gilbert. He might have even followed her to the warehouse.

But before she could make sense of any of it, she heard music emanating from the back yard.

After walking into the kitchen, she pulled back the curtain on the window above the sink. In the darkness, she could just make out a tent and one of those outdoor patio heaters shaped like a round chimney. Puzzled, she walked out the back door, the squeaking hinges announcing her arrival.

Zach stood at the grill, marinating two steaks with a brush. The aroma of sizzling meat made her mouth water.

"What are you doing out here?" she asked him.

"Well, I'm supposed to be on vacation," he said,

flipping over one of the steaks. "And I've always wanted to camp out, so I thought I'd give it a try."

"Camping?" She looked at the tent, then the stone chimney. It had a small fire burning in it, just enough to cast a romantic glow over the lawn. "Here? In my back yard?"

He fixed his gaze on the grill. "I figured we'd both have a little more room this way. I was going a little stir crazy in the house."

His face was flushed, though she couldn't tell if it was from the heat of the grill or something else.

"Besides," he continued, "Texas is a lot different than Boston. I can actually see the stars out here."

She looked up at the sky, impressed with the glittering canopy above her. After living in Kendall so long, she'd taken sights like that for granted. "It is beautiful, isn't it?"

"Breathtaking," he agreed. But Zach wasn't looking at the sky—he was looking straight at her.

Relief that he hadn't left her mingled with guilt that she wasn't telling him about finding Gilbert or about her plan to meet him tomorrow night. But something told her now wasn't the time.

"Are you hungry?" he asked, taking off the steaks.

Famished. But for more than food. That was something else she didn't tell him as he led her to the tent, carrying the meat on a platter. He had cushions on the canvas floor with small table set up between them.

Two place settings of her aunt's fine china were set on the table, along with a neatly folded linen napkin. Merlot sparkled in the wineglasses and a taper candle burned in the center of the table, casting a flickering golden glow inside the tent.

"Looks like you've thought of everything," she said, taking a seat across from him, "except silverware."

He smiled, then pulled two forks and two steak knives out of his pocket. "Hey, I used to be a Boy Scout. I'm always prepared."

She laughed, realizing there was something different about him. He was more relaxed, the tiny tension lines erased from his eyes and mouth.

"Dig in." He handed her a linen napkin, then laid his own across his lap.

She picked up the knife and fork, eyeing the steak in front of her. "There's no way I can eat all of this."

"Just make sure you save room for dessert," he replied. "We're roasting marshmallows."

She picked up her fork. "So were you really a Boy Scout?"

"For a couple of years," Zach said, cutting into his steak, "until my dad left and I had to find a job. But I never did get to go on any campouts."

Gracie found she enjoyed talking with Zach about something other than the case and Gilbert, two subjects that had dominated their every conversation for the past few days. She wanted to savor this moment, make it a special memory she could keep forever and dust off once in a while whenever her life got too mundane.

"More wine?" He refilled her glass before she even had a chance to reply, then topped off his own.

They ate and talked, oblivious to everything but each other. Zach told her about growing up in south Boston and why he'd decided to become a cop. Gracie talked about her parents and how abandoned she'd felt when they'd left her—something she'd never even confided to Gilbert.

She never wanted the evening to end. Looking around her back yard, Gracie felt as though she and Zach were alone in the world. *If only it were true.* "I've never done anything like this before."

"Neither have I," he admitted. "Paul gave me the idea."

"Paul?" she echoed. "Paul Toscano?"

He nodded, then pushed his empty plate away. "He's a nice guy. I like him."

"When did you see Paul?"

"At the bookstore today when I went looking for you."

"About that…" she began, still uncertain how much to tell him.

"Later," he said, then held out his hand. "It's time for dessert."

She let him pull her to her feet. They just stood there for a moment together, their shadows touching on the tent wall. Gracie looked up at Zach, suddenly hoping that he'd kiss her.

Instead he handed her a stick with the bark peeled off. "Made especially for you."

She laughed, then stuck a marshmallow on the end of the stick while he carried the small table, the dishes still on top of it, into the kitchen. When he emerged from the house, Zach peeled a stick of his own before joining her by the stone chimney.

"How much did all of this cost?" she asked, standing next to him as they roasted the marshmallows.

"The sticks were free," he replied. "I pilfered them from your yard."

"And the rest?"

He turned to look at her. "The rest doesn't matter. It was worth every penny."

Something in his eyes told her this night was just beginning. A thrill of anticipation shot through her and Gracie knew exactly what she wanted for dessert.

"You're marshmallow's burning," he said softly. Zach pulled her stick toward him and blew out the fire. Then he carefully pulled the marshmallow off and held it to her mouth. "Be careful. It might be hot."

She grasped his hand, bringing it closer to her mouth. Then she lightly blew on it before taking a tiny nibble of the charred surface. The gooey, warm middle oozed out and she caught it with her tongue.

She saw Zach watching her and noticed his eyes darken when her tongue flicked over his thumb. Taking her time, she took small bites of the marshmallow, enjoying both the sweet flavor and Zach's reaction. When it was gone, she brought his fingers to her mouth.

She'd been wanting to touch him, to taste him, since that day in the cabin. Now, she circled her tongue around each fingertip, her gaze never leaving his face. Then she drew his index finger deeper into her mouth, simulating an act that made his breathing grow heavy.

She slid her tongue around it, easing his finger in and out of her mouth until every last trace of marshmallow was gone. Then she repeated the act with each remaining finger, ending with his thumb. By that time, Zach's arousal was evident in the glow of the fire.

"That was delicious," she said, feeling a little stickiness on her lower lip as she spoke. She reached up to wipe it off, but Zach stopped her.

"Let me," he rasped.

He leaned forward, nipping her lip with his mouth until the stickiness was gone.

"We still have mine," he said, pulling his marshmallow from the fire. It was charred almost beyond recognition, but neither one of them seemed to mind.

Gracie pulled it off and brought the marshmallow to his lips, then replaced it with her mouth. Zach moaned low in his throat, his arms coming around her.

But she placed her hands flat on his chest, pushing him gently back onto the blanket inside the tent. He pulled her with him, her body sprawled on top of his. She could feel the hard ridge of his erection between her thighs and the rapid beat of his heart beneath her hands.

"Now I have you exactly where I want you," she breathed.

"The question is," he said softly, "what are you going to do with me?"

"You'll see, Zach," she promised. "You'll see."

13

ZACH STARED up at Gracie, wondering if she had any idea how exquisite she looked in the light of the fire. The glow made golden highlights shine in her hair and made her eyes such a deep blue that he could happily drown in their depths.

He watched her reach up and start opening her blouse, one button at a time. She moved with excruciating slowness until every nerve fiber in his body vibrated with anticipation. After what seemed an eternity, she slipped out of her blouse, her breasts almost spilling out of the top of her lacy white bra.

The urge to reach out and touch them almost overwhelmed him, but he made himself wait, wanting to see what Gracie was going to do next. She sat up on her knees, braced on either side of his hips, then popped open the top button of her slacks. She wriggled out of them, rising to her feet and lifting one leg, then the other, to pull them off.

Zach's breath caught in his throat as she towered above him, still straddling his hips, but wearing nothing except her bra and panties. From his vantage point, her slender legs seemed to go on forever, stretching up to that thatch of white silk that concealed his ultimate destination.

But before he could begin the journey, she lowered herself once more, her face now hovering just above his waistband. He groaned as she bent her mouth to his groin, feeling her warm breath through the denim fabric of his jeans. Then her lips made contact and he knew the meaning of paradise.

The sensation almost undid him. He grabbed fistfuls of the blanket beneath him as she moved up and down, creating a friction so hot he thought he might explode.

When he couldn't take it anymore, he sat up and grasped her shoulders, pulling her up for a soul-wrenching kiss. Her hands pulled his shirt out of the waistband of his jeans, buttons flying as she tore it open.

He cradled her face in his hands, showering kisses on her mouth, her nose, her cheeks. Savoring the feel of her soft skin and the heady taste of her that he knew would leave him craving more.

Sometime in that vortex of desire, he shed his jeans and underwear, then watched her remove her bra and panties while he rolled on a condom. Then he lay with her on the blanket, her skin feeling like silk against him. Zach caressed her cheek with one knuckle, ignoring the pounding need in his body to savor this moment together.

"You are so beautiful," he breathed.

Tears gleamed in her eyes, but she smiled at his

words. "I'm glad you weren't Gilbert. That night at the reunion. I'm glad it was you."

"Me, too," he said, settling into the warm cradle of her body. He intended to take his time, lowering his head to nuzzle each breast. His tongue circled one nipple then the other, drawing sweet whimpers of desire from her throat.

Then her hands moved on him and he knew that time was something he didn't have. As if sensing his need, she opened her legs for him. An invitation he couldn't resist.

The next moment he was inside of her, relishing the way she enveloped him. Her warmth. Her acceptance. Then she moved her hips, arching upwards, driving him to the brink of ecstasy. His body began to move of its own volition, driven by a need that almost scared him

He needed Gracie. A fact he embraced now, just as he embraced her, catching her mouth in a kiss as their bodies moved together, harder and faster, until they both reached a crescendo that made them cry out into the night.

"Zach!"

This time she called out *his* name. Satisfaction, deep and primal, flowed through him. His woman. His love.

His Gracie.

THE NEXT MORNING, Gracie awoke in her bed, the sun slanting through her window. She lay wrapped in Zach's arms, his warm body spooned around her back and his head nestled in the crook of her shoulder.

He'd carried her inside the house when lightning had flashed across the sky in the middle of the night. Then he'd made love to her again as the thunder boomed and raindrops pattered against the window-pane. She could still taste marshmallow on her tongue. And Zach. A thrill shot through her at the memory of their night together.

A night that had burned away her last remaining doubts about trusting him.

"Are you awake?" she whispered.

"Hmmm," he murmured against her neck.

"Zach," she said, turning in his arms to face him.

His eyes were half closed, his face slack with sleep. "I'm awake."

She smiled, hating to rouse him from his relaxed state. But this was too important to wait. "It's about Gilbert."

His eyes opened at the name, tension lines forming around his mouth. "What about him?"

Gracie wasn't sure how to broach the subject without making him angry, so she just decided to tell him straight out instead of trying to sugarcoat it. "I saw him, Zach."

"You what?" He was wide awake now, rising up on one elbow. "When?"

She placed one hand on his shoulder, smoothing it over the taut muscles there. "Last night. Right before I came home. I met him at an abandoned warehouse on Parvey Road."

He stared at her for a moment, then pulled her tight against him. "Promise me you'll never do that again, Gracie. He could have hurt you or...worse."

Her eyes stung at the anguish she heard in his voice. "I'm fine," she assured him. "Gilbert would never hurt me. He just wanted to talk to me."

Zach held her a few moments longer before finally pulling away far enough to look into her face. "So what did he say to you?"

She sighed, part of her feeling like she was betraying her friend. But she couldn't keep this secret from Zach any longer. Not after what had happened between them last night.

"He wants me to bring him the videotape."

Zach sat up at that news, muscles flexing in his chest at the movement. Gracie couldn't help staring at his body, honed to perfection. He seemed oblivious to the effect looking at him had on her. Or maybe he was used to women ogling him in bed.

She shook that unpleasant thought from her head. He was with *her* at this moment. That's all that mattered. She couldn't let herself worry about yesterday or tomorrow, not when she knew how often life interfered with her plans.

But part of her couldn't help but dream about a future with Zach, making love with him every night, waking up with him every morning. A dream that seemed impossible with so many obstacles in their way—but that didn't make it any less precious.

"That damn tape," Zach muttered. "What's on it that could be so important?"

She shook her head. "Gilbert wouldn't tell me, though he did say that he intended to take it straight to the police."

Zach arched a skeptical brow. "And you believed him?"

A chill passed through her at his expression. "Of course. He'd never lie to me."

He tossed back the covers and climbed out of her bed. "I don't believe this. Why didn't you tell me all of this right away?"

She pulled the sheet up to her chest, hating the tension forming between them once more. The same tired argument. Zach vilifying Gilbert while she defended him. She didn't want any more walls between them, but he had to at least meet her halfway.

"I wasn't going to tell you at all," she replied, watching him get dressed. "But..."

"But?" he prodded, then his face softened. "But you thought I wouldn't be such a jerk about it." He walked over to the bed and reached for her hands. "Look, Gracie, I'm not really upset with you. Just the thought of you alone with that guy...." He grasped her hands tighter. "Anything could have happened."

"Don't you trust me?" she asked, really needing to know the answer.

"Yes," he replied without hesitation. "It's Holloway I don't trust."

"But I've told you over and over that Gilbert would never hurt me. If I matter to you at all," she said, meeting his gaze, "then you need to know how important it is for you to believe me."

"You matter," he said firmly. "You have no idea how much. Gracie, I…" The phone rang, cutting off his words. He huffed out a breath, then said, "I'll get it."

When Zach walked out the door, Gracie climbed out of bed and got dressed. She could hear his voice in the other room, surprised the phone call hadn't been for her. Who would be calling Zach at her house?

She discovered the answer to the question when he walked back into her bedroom. "It was the Kendall police. They have Dorie in custody. Apparently she wants to cut a deal."

"In custody?" Gracie said. "How did that happen?"

"She stole a car and was headed out of town when it broke down. The police caught up with her before she could get away."

"She was leaving Kendall?"

"Looks that way."

"Then Allison's plan must have fallen through. That means Gilbert could be in trouble."

"Forget about Gilbert," he bit out. "I want you to promise me to stay away from both him and that warehouse until I get back from the police station."

"But—"

"No, Gracie. We have to do this my way. If we're lucky, Dorie will spill everything and we'll be able to wrap up this case today."

After everything she'd said, everything that had happened between them, Zach was still acting solo. He didn't really trust her. Didn't believe in her. And it was starting to seem likely he'd never be able to do either. So much for fantasizing about a future with him. It was just another dream that wouldn't come true.

"Promise me," he prodded, his gaze intent on her face.

She looked at him, something breaking inside of her. "All right."

He leaned over to kiss her, his hands gripping her shoulders. "I'll be back as soon as I can. Then we'll talk about everything. About us."

Gracie watched him walk out the door, knowing nothing would ever be the same between them.

Because she was about to break a promise to the man she loved.

ZACH DIDN'T realize until he entered the Kendall Police Station that he'd forgotten the videotape. He'd been too distracted by the expression on Gracie's face to think clearly. Something was wrong, but he wouldn't be able to resolve it until he cleared up this mess with Gilbert.

Holloway was the problem, as always. Coming between them just when they were about to make a connection. Like this morning, when he'd awakened to find himself in Gracie's bed. For a moment, he thought it had been a dream. Then she'd smiled at him and he'd known it was real.

That's why this uneasiness roiling around inside of him bothered Zach so much. He felt as if he were being pulled in two different directions, forced to choose between doing his duty as a cop and making Gracie happy.

It was also the reason he needed to close this case before it broke them apart. He wanted Gracie to be his first priority. Wanted to give her his full and undivided attention.

But that wasn't the only reason. Despite Gracie's promise to stay away from Holloway, he couldn't really be sure she appreciated the danger she was in. She was so confident in her ability to judge people, especially Gilbert. His partner had been the same way before he'd been shot. So sure he could handle any situation.

But he'd been wrong.

And Zach had been wrong to ignore his own instincts just to make Ray happy. He'd lost a partner because of Gilbert Holloway. So he wasn't about to take the chance of losing Gracie.

"Detective Maddox?"

He turned around to see Sergeant Hayes walking toward him, wearing wrinkled gray slacks and a white shirt with a blue tie. He carried a cup of coffee in his hand, along with a chocolate donut wrapped in a paper napkin.

"Glad you could make it on such short notice," Hayes said, stopping beside him.

"I just hope this won't take long."

"We're still waiting for Dorie Phillips's lawyer to show up." He held up the doughnut. "I figured there would be enough time for me to have breakfast."

Impatience wafted through him. "She lawyered up already?"

"She's a smart one," Hayes said, taking a sip of his

coffee. "Smart enough to know she's got information we can use. I think you'll be happy you came down here."

But Zach was already regretting it. Lawyers were notorious for causing delays, not only in criminal trials, but in every other aspect of the justice system. He'd always figured Delays 101 was a required course in law school.

Now he'd have to bide his time here while Gracie waited for him alone at the house. At least she'd promised to stay put, so he wouldn't have to worry about her.

Thirty minutes later, Hayes tracked him down at the coffee machine. "The lawyer finally showed up. He and Dorie are in conference right now, but that shouldn't take too long. Then you can talk to her."

Zach had waited six months for this case to be over, so he figured he could wait a few minutes more.

But it was more than an hour before he was finally called into the interrogation room. Dorie sat at the table beside her lawyer, looking tired and sullen. Her attorney was a young man, fresh out of law school, judging by the new leather aroma of his briefcase.

"My client is willing to offer information in a criminal case in exchange for a plea deal," the attorney said. "I think you'll find it worth your while."

"Let's hear what she has to say first," Zach said.

Dorie's head jerked up at the sound of his voice. "Are you from Boston?"

He nodded, surprised his accent was that noticeable. "That's right. I've been working on the Holloway case for several months now."

Her mouth thinned. "Gilbert Holloway is to blame for all of this. He roped us in, making us believe he was legit. Then it was too late to back out."

"Who's we?" Zach asked.

"My cousin Allison and I," Dorie replied. "She'll back me up if my word's not good enough. I know she will."

Zach pulled out a chair and sat down, ready to get down to business. "Then tell me where she and Holloway are hiding."

Dorie snorted. "They're not together. Gilbert doesn't trust her enough to let her hide out with him. He doesn't trust anybody."

Except Gracie.

Zach's instincts told him she wasn't safe, no matter how much she protested to the contrary. Or maybe it was the thought of losing her that made him refuse to believe her about Holloway. She was so damn loyal to the man.

"Here's the thing," Dorie said, glancing at her lawyer. "I don't want to do any jail time. I've made too many enemies, inside and out. If I agree to testify against Holloway at his trial, then I want full immunity."

"I think you're getting ahead of yourself," Zach said. "We're not making any deals until both Holloway and Allison are in custody."

She shrugged. "Fine. I just hope you don't keep

wasting time with that Dawson woman, because Gilbert is planning to leave the country today."

That Dawson woman. The way she said it, like acid dripping from her tongue, made his skin prickle. "How do you know about Gracie?"

Dorie rolled her eyes. "Allison doesn't take any chances. She knows Gilbert has a soft spot for the woman. So she's been watching the house and knows you've been staying there. The only thing she doesn't know is that you're a cop. She figured Gilbert brought Gracie in on the deal and you were just another guy who would get a split of the pot."

Zach hesitated, wondering how much he should reveal to Dorie. Then again, she wasn't going anywhere. "How can Gilbert be leaving today if he's got a meeting set up with Gracie tonight?"

Dorie laughed out loud. "You people are so dense! This is why he's still on the loose. There is no meeting tonight. It's all a scam."

Zach stared at her, certain Gracie wouldn't lie to him. Still, there'd been something in her eyes this morning.... "How do you know?"

"Because I was there, in the warehouse, when Gilbert's little Gracie came calling. I heard everything. He set her up, making her believe the tape had some secret message. It's simply bait for Allison. She's the one he wants to frame for all of this."

"So Allison's the one meeting her tonight?"

Dorie nodded. "Why else would he make it so easy for you?"

She had a point, though Gilbert hadn't known

Gracie would tell a cop about the meeting. *Or had he?* Maybe Gracie had told him all about Zach staying with her. He raked his hand through his hair, uncertain what to believe.

The lawyer rose to his feet. "Sounds like my client has given you more than enough information for that plea deal."

Zach looked at Sergeant Hayes. "This isn't my jurisdiction, so it's not my call."

Hayes hesitated for a moment, then gave a brisk nod. "You've got a deal, but we won't make it official until we bring this Webb woman into custody."

"Just send me the paperwork," the lawyer said. Then he left the interrogation room along with Dorie, who was escorted by a guard.

Hayes turned to Zach. "So what can our department do to help you?"

It was a sticky jurisdictional problem. Gilbert Holloway hadn't broken any laws in Texas. Yet. But they had enough evidence to suspect him of a possible conspiracy, along with Allison Webb, and she did live in this jurisdiction.

"Nothing until tonight," Zach replied. "That's when Gracie's supposed to meet Gilbert at the warehouse, although it sounds like Allison is the one who will show up. Maybe you could send a couple of unmarked cars out that way to intercept her."

Hayes nodded. "No problem. Is there anything else you need?"

"As a matter of fact, there is." Zach stood up and

moved toward the door. "But let me buy you lunch first. I'm starving."

Hayes laughed. "I never turn down a free meal. Lead the way."

Zach glanced at his watch, hoping to make it a quick meal. He wanted to get back to Gracie. And if everything proceeded as planned, he'd never have to leave her again.

14

GRACIE WORKED on autopilot that morning at the bookstore. She shelved the latest arrivals, assisted customers, and caught up with the paperwork while her mind was somewhere else. On Zach, to be exact. And on the videotape in her purse.

If only she knew what was on it.

"Earth to Gracie," Trina said, a sharp edge to her voice.

She blinked, then looked up from her desk. "Oh, sorry. What do you need?"

"The stapler," Trina snapped. She'd been in a bad mood all morning, snarling at customers and even avoiding the phone.

"I've asked you for it three times already."

Gracie plucked the stapler off the desk and handed it to her. "I guess I'm not quite with it today."

"Not getting enough sleep these days with that sexy cop living at your house? Must be rough."

Her mind flashed to making love with Zach in the tent, then later in her bed. She'd been so sure everything had been resolved between them. But obviously good sex, no *great* sex, couldn't solve everything.

"Do you want to tell me what's bothering you?" Gracie asked, finally confronting Trina's attitude. "Or do you want to just keep growling at me and everybody else who walks through the door?"

Trina's mouth thinned, then she turned away. "Sorry. I've just remembered that my life sucks and I can't do a damn thing about it."

That didn't sound like Trina. She was not a woman to feel sorry for herself.

"What's wrong?" Gracie prodded. "Maybe you'll feel better if you tell me."

"What's right?" she countered, then heaved a long sigh. "Forget it. I'd rather hear what's going on with you. Why are you so out of it today?"

Gracie knew Trina was avoiding the issue, but she also knew better than to push her. Trina would confide her problems when she was good and ready. Gracie, on the other hand, needed some answers now.

"I can't stop thinking about Zach," she began. "I believe he cares about me, maybe even loves me. But he hasn't been able to rely on anyone but himself for so long that he doesn't know how to trust—or how to admit when he's wrong."

Trina winced. "Not exactly the best basis for a relationship."

"I know." Gracie glanced over then filed an invoice. "The worst part is that I still want him in my life, inner warts and all."

"So go for it," Trina said.

Gracie wished it was that easy. But Gilbert was still standing between them. As much as she loved

Zach, she couldn't compromise her values. And one of those values was loyalty. Gilbert had been her best friend for over a decade and even though they'd gone their separate ways, he needed her now. She couldn't turn her back on him.

Something that Zach would never understand.

"Not to change the subject," Trina said, looking around the store. "But have you heard from Paul today?"

"No. Isn't he here?"

"I haven't seen him all morning."

"Maybe he's sick," Gracie ventured.

"He's never sick. The guy hasn't missed a day here for the past three years." Trina shuffled a stack of receipts in front of her. "Besides, I called his house. There was no answer."

Gracie smiled. "So you do have a soft spot for him after all."

Trina grimaced. "Please. I'm just concerned, that's all. Something happened last night and, well, I may have said some things that hurt him…" Her voice trailed off and she pressed her lips together.

"For two people constantly surrounded by romance books, we both certainly seem to have trouble in that department. You'd think we'd have learned something by now."

"None of those books have anyone with a disability for a hero or heroine," Trina retorted. "They're all perfect. You talked about Zach's inner warts." She pointed to her prosthesis. "Well, I have an outer wart that no man can overlook."

At least now Gracie knew the cause of Trina's mood. Despite her denial, Paul did mean something to her. Trina just wasn't ready to believe that any man could love her.

"First of all," Gracie said, "you're wrong about those perfect heroes and heroines. There's a Harlequin Temptation called *Out of the Darkness* with a hero who is disfigured by a fire. And another one called *Tongue-Tied*, that has a heroine with a speech disability."

"They're fiction, though, aren't they?" Trina said wryly. "Not real life."

"Second of all," Gracie continued as if she hadn't spoken, "Paul does care about you, despite your 'wart.' That's obvious to anyone who sees you two together."

Trina set her jaw. "He just feels sorry for me. Why else would he offer to help me so much? I'm not going to be with any man out of pity."

"You know, I saw one of his poems once," Gracie said softly. "It was about you, Trina. He compared you to the sun and how he needed to orbit around you to feel light and warmth in his world. It was beautiful."

Her face softened. "A poem? Why didn't he ever show it to me?"

"I don't know," Gracie replied. "Maybe he was afraid of your reaction. Sometimes dreams are safer than reality."

The truth of her own words hit her in the solar plexus. How long had she dreamed of law school, yet always found some excuse not to pursue it? Yes, she had obligations, but so did most people. They still found a way to make their dreams come true.

"I need to get out of here for a while," Trina said, grabbing her purse. "If you need me, I'll be over at Temptation having a drink or three."

"All right." Gracie watched her walk out the door. The limp was more pronounced than ever today, but she knew Trina's real handicap was the way she saw herself.

Maybe Gracie had the same problem. Seeing obstacles where none really existed. Was it possible for her to go to law school and run the bookstore? Had she been holding back not out of necessity, but out of fear?

There was certainly a basis for that fear—like racking up big debts and juggling her life around. Yet, part of her was ready to throw caution to the wind and just go for it, knowing full well there wouldn't be any guarantees.

The fact that she was even considering such a thing surprised her. But deep down Gracie knew she was more than considering it. She was going to do it.

The bell on the door jingled and she looked up to see Paul walk inside. She almost didn't recognize him. He'd shaved his beard and wore a new gray suit.

"Well, look at you," Gracie said as Paul walked up to the counter. "What's the occasion?"

A grin prefaced his announcement. "I sold my book."

"You did?" Gracie rounded the counter and embraced him in a hug. "Paul, that's wonderful!"

"I still can't believe it. The editor called me this morning and gave me the good news. I've been pinching myself ever since."

"So that's why you were a no-show when we opened today. Trina and I were wondering what happened to you."

His grin faded. "I'm surprised Trina noticed. In fact, I thought it would be less uncomfortable for both of us if I stayed away from now on. But I had to come in and share the news."

Trina had mentioned something happening between them last night, but Gracie hadn't thought it actually serious enough to drive Paul away. "What's happened?"

He looked surprised. "She didn't tell you?"

"Not specifically."

"I proposed to her last night."

Gracie stared at him, waiting for the punch line. "Proposed...marriage?"

He nodded. "She had the same look on her face that you do. Best described as stunned disbelief."

"You two have never even dated. Don't you think a proposal was a little premature?"

Resolution darkened his eyes. "You know what, Gracie? I've been hopelessly in love with that woman for the past three years, as she was well aware. I thought it was time to declare myself and see where I stood. Now I know."

Gracie wanted to shake both of them. "Paul, I'm

sure your proposal came as a shock to Trina. Give her some time to think about it. She might not be ready for marriage, but…"

He shook his head. "Look, I'm not here to talk about my disaster of a love life. I have an offer I hope you can't refuse."

"What kind of offer?"

"I'd like to invest in Between the Covers, if you don't mind taking on a partner."

She stared at him, shocked into silence.

"I've got a big advance coming my way," he said with a wide grin. "So, what better way to invest that money than in a business that showcases my work? Between the Covers is like a second home to me. I won't be coming here anymore, but I'd still like to be a part of it."

"I don't know what to say."

"Say yes," he insisted. "I've already found a prime spot for us to relocate. It's a little pricey, but I'd like the lease to be my investment. We can work out all the financial details later. I'm willing to defer the return on my investment until the new store is up and running."

Gracie had never subscribed in mystical mumbo-jumbo, but this almost made her a believer. Only moments before, she'd made the decision to pursue her dream of becoming a lawyer despite the obstacles in her way. Then Paul had walked in the door and removed the biggest roadblock.

"Just think about it," Paul entreated. "We can go look at the site tomorrow and you can give me your decision then."

"I don't have to think about it," Gracie replied, holding out her hand. "Partner."

"You mean it?" he exclaimed, then let out a whoop as he grabbed her hand and pumped it up and down.

"On one condition." Gracie hoped she wasn't overstepping the bounds of her friendship with Trina and Paul.

Paul beamed at her. "Just name it."

"Don't give up on Trina yet. Talk to her—at least one more time. She's over at Temptation right now having a drink."

He looked more resigned than perturbed by her suggestion. "It will just be a waste of time."

"Just go." She pushed him toward the door. "I'll start drawing up a rough draft of our agreement while you're over there."

"This shouldn't take long," Paul said, walking out of the bookstore.

Gracie stared after him, still awed by the sudden turn her life had just taken. She'd never imagined that Paul could hold the key to solving her problem with the bookstore. And he'd been right in front of her eyes the whole time.

Right in front of her eyes.

Maybe she'd been looking at the videotape the wrong way, too. She walked back to her desk and pulled it out of her purse. After watching it a hundred times, she still had no clue why it was so important to Gilbert. But what if the reason wasn't *on* the tape. What if it was *inside* the tape?

There was only one way to find out.

ZACH WALKED into Temptation, his eyes adjusting to the dim lighting inside. The cool air was a welcome respite from the hot afternoon sun. A beer would taste even better.

He walked over to the bar and took a seat on a barstool. A young woman stood at the door of the kitchen, talking to a man in a white apron that read Hot and Spicy.

From the color of her hair and eyes, Zach guessed she must be Cat Sheehan, one of the bar owners. No doubt the older man standing in the doorway was Zeke Watson, who worked the grill.

Strange how he knew them so well when he'd never met them before. Their physical attributes matched Gracie's e-mail descriptions perfectly. With such strong communication skills, she'd make a damn good lawyer if she ever got the chance.

Zach wanted to help her have that chance—and more. But he had to find her first.

"May I help you?" Cat said, moving toward him.

"I'd like a Michelob on tap if you have it," Zach replied, "and some information."

"The beer I can handle." Cat grabbed a frosty mug from the cooler and walked over to the tap. "The information depends on the subject."

"The subject is Gracie Dawson."

Her eyes grew wide, and then she looked him up and down. "Let me guess, you're the cop who's been staying at her house."

"That's right."

She nodded. "Gracie's told me a lot about you."

He wondered just how much, but the expression on Cat's face made it clear that she wasn't going to tell.

"I was just over at Between the Covers," he began, "but it's closed. I was hoping you might know where I could find Gracie."

"Closed?" Cat crinkled her brow. "That's odd. I can't ever remember the bookstore closing in the middle of the afternoon. Somebody is always there."

"That's what I thought," Zach took a deep sip of his beer. "Paul was there the last time I stopped by."

Her brow cleared as a smile teased her mouth. "Well, that could explain it."

"What do you mean?"

"Paul and Trina were in here about an hour ago. When they left, I should have guessed they weren't going back to the bookstore."

"Why do you say that?"

She leaned over the counter, lowering her voice. "Let's just say they barely made it out the door with their clothes on. First they were talking, then they were arguing, then they were kissing. I'm talking H-O-T. I never knew that Toscano guy had it in him."

Score one for Paul. Zach smiled into his beer mug before taking another sip. At least that explained why the bookstore was closed. Gracie probably had to run out for a few minutes and had no one there to run the place.

"Oh, by the way," Cat said, wiping the counter in front of him. "If you hurt, Gracie, I'll kill you."

Zach set down his beer mug. He admired her loyalty, even if he was at the receiving end of her threat. "I have no intention of hurting her."

"Glad to hear it."

He finished his beer, then fished his wallet out of his back pocket.

"The beer's on me," Cat said, picking up the empty mug. "Just tell Gracie to stop in sometime soon. I have a lot to tell her."

He nodded, putting his wallet away. "Thanks."

When he emerged from the bar, he glanced at Between the Covers, hoping to find it open once more. But the Closed sign was still on the door, evoking a twinge of anxiety deep inside of him.

Gracie was right. He worried too much. The Holloway case was almost wrapped up and his life was finally on the right track. All he had to do was nab Gilbert and the man would be out of Gracie's life forever.

Leaving plenty of room for Zach to step in.

15

GRACIE STOOD outside the Kendall State Bank, staring at the silver key in her hand and wondering if she should continue to follow her instincts.

She'd been right about the video, finding the key taped on the inside of the cassette case. Now the question was where this key would lead her. Gracie needed to know the answer before she met with Gilbert. The tape was ruined now, since she'd been unable to put it back together after prying it open. And she wasn't about to just hand over the key.

Especially since she had a good idea where to find the lock that it opened.

Twelve years ago, she'd been with Gilbert when he'd leased a safe-deposit box at this very bank. He'd just started a computer repair business and planned to keep the income separate from his checking account so he wouldn't be tempted to spend all his earnings.

Gracie had forgotten all about it until she'd found the key. It was smaller than a house key, looking almost identical to the one kept by her aunt for her safe-deposit box at the same bank.

Even after all these years, she hadn't forgotten the

number to Gilbert's box. He'd laughed when the bank clerk had assigned the number to him, saying all he had to do was think of Gracie's June tenth birthday to remember the number.

Gracie swallowed a sigh, realizing how different Gilbert was then from the man she'd seen in the warehouse. More open and easygoing, less paranoid and tense. The years hadn't been good to him.

Though, she supposed hiding out from the police, as well as the people who wanted to shut him up, could do that to a man. Gracie just wished he'd confided in her sooner. Maybe she could have found some way to help him.

She still might have that chance now.

Taking a deep breath, she walked inside the bank, wondering how she was going to convince them to let her have access to that safe-deposit box when she didn't even have an account here.

Then she saw her old classmate Sandra Atley standing behind one of the teller windows. As a new employee, she probably didn't know all the bank's customers yet. As an avid gossip, she might be willing to bend the rules in exchange for some juicy information.

"Well, hello there," Sandra said as Gracie walked up to her window. "You disappeared from the reunion the other night. What happened?"

"Gilbert and I wanted to reminisce in private."

Sandra heaved a wistful sigh. "Lucky you. I was hoping for a chance to *reminisce* with him myself, but I guess you had first dibs."

Gracie leaned closer. "Actually it turns out he wasn't Gilbert."

Her eyes widened. "What?"

"He was a policeman from Boston impersonating Gilbert as part of a criminal investigation."

"No way!"

"It's true," Gracie said. "I don't know all the details, but Allison Webb is involved."

"Well, that's no surprise," Sandra replied. "That woman never was up to any good." Then she reached for the cordless phone in front of her. "I've got to call my mother. She'll just flip when she hears this."

Gracie held up the key in her hand. "I need to check a safe-deposit box."

"Oh, sure," Sandra replied, handing over the prep key that fit in all the boxes.

Gracie knew a safe-deposit box couldn't be opened by one key alone. That was part of the bank's security feature. The prep key had to be inserted first, then the key she'd found in the videotape could open the box. *If* her instincts were right about it.

"Just bring back the prep key when you're through," Sandra said, already punching in the numbers on her phone.

It had been easier than Gracie had imagined.

A moment later she stood inside the vault, her gaze scanning the rows upon rows of safe-deposit boxes until she saw the number she wanted: 610.

She walked over to the box, a knot in her stomach, then inserted the prep key into the lock, followed by the key she'd found in the cassette. A soft click sounded, then the box popped open.

She pulled it out and set it on the table, her heart thudding in her chest. Was there cash in there? Precious jewels? Drugs or other contraband? Ready for anything, she opened the lid. But Gracie wasn't prepared for what she saw inside.

It was a computer disk.

The flat, gray 3.5 inch floppy disk looked like any other computer disk. She picked it up, turning it over in her hand. Another mystery. But this time she knew it wouldn't take her as long to figure it out. All she had to do was go home and fire up her computer.

And figure out what she was going to tell Zach.

But her time ran out when Zach met her at the door of her house.

"Where have you been?" he asked, pulling her into his arms. "I was starting to worry."

Her traitorous body savored his warmth, despite knowing she might never trust him enough to be someone she wanted in her life. Zach seemed perfect for her in so many ways. But the greatest test was yet to come.

"I stopped by the bank on my way home." She stepped out of his arms. "I figured out the secret of the videotape, Zach."

He smiled. "I know how hard you've worked on this, Gracie, but there is no secret. Dorie Phillips confessed that it was all a ruse."

She pulled the computer disk out of her purse. "Then why did I find a key inside the tape cassette?

A key that opened a security deposit box at the Kendall State Bank with this disk in it?"

His brow creased as he took the disk from her. "What the hell is this?"

"It's proof that I was right about Gilbert. Allison and Dorie are the ones pulling the ruse, trying to set him up to take the blame for everything."

Zach shook his head. "We don't know that for sure."

"Then let's put this in my computer and find out. I have a feeling that everything we need to know is right here."

Thirty minutes later, Gracie was proven right.

"Holloway's got it all," Zach said, scrolling through the pages of information the computer screen. "Everything we need to file charges. Names. Dates. Every transaction that's connected to the credit card thefts. Gilbert must have saved it all to this disk before erasing it from his hard drive. We've spent months looking for this stuff."

Gracie couldn't believe it was almost over. "It's pretty clear that Allison and Dorie were the ones stealing the numbers. Either to use for themselves or to sell to the highest bidder. Gilbert was the gullible middleman."

Zach turned in his chair, taking her hands in his own. "All this proves is that Gilbert wanted some insurance. Dorie told us that he's the mastermind behind this entire scheme."

Gracie wanted to scream. After everything that had happened between them, he still wouldn't budge from his misconception about Gilbert. He still wouldn't believe in her.

"You're wrong," she told him. "But the only way I can prove it to you is by going to that warehouse tonight and confronting Gilbert."

Zach's face softened. "Sweetheart, Gilbert's not even going to be there. It's all a setup. Allison is supposed to arrive at the same time you do. It's not safe, Gracie. That woman hates you."

"Gilbert wouldn't do that to me." Gracie cupped Zach's face with her hands, entreating him to believe in her. "If you care about me at all, you'll let me do this. Maybe Gilbert isn't completely innocent in all of this, but I want to help him. As his friend, that's the least I can do."

Anguish shone in Zach's dark eyes. She knew she was putting him in a difficult position—making him prove his love for her by letting her do something he thought might be risky. But Gracie didn't have any other choice. She couldn't plan a future with him if he couldn't agree to meet her halfway.

"Damn it, Gracie, don't ask me to do this. I can't let you go in there alone. Not after what happened to Ray."

"I'll be fine," she promised him. "I'm not Ray. And Gilbert's not the one who shot him. You've got to trust me on this, Zach."

He didn't say anything for so long that she almost gave up hope. Then he met her gaze and the expression in her eyes told her that she'd won.

"You have to wear a wire," he bit out, "so I can

hear what's going on inside. The second I think it's too dangerous, I'm coming in. Understand?"

She leaned forward and gently kissed his lips, aware of how difficult this was for him. "Perfectly. Do you understand how much this means to me?"

He pulled her to him, his embrace so tight she could barely breathe. "I must be crazy to let you do this."

For the first time, Gracie wavered in her conviction of Gilbert's innocence. If he was guilty as Zach believed, then she was putting her loyalty to him above the man she loved. But at this point, she didn't have a choice.

"I hate to say it." Zach pulled away from her. "But we'd better go."

She nodded, then took a deep breath. Soon she'd know which one of them was right about Gilbert. She just hoped their relationship could survive the outcome.

A LIGHT RAIN FELL as Gracie stood a few blocks from the warehouse, letting Zach adjust her jacket around the wire she wore to record her conversation with whomever showed up—either Gilbert or Allison.

Four other Kendall police officers stood nearby, talking quietly to each other around their unmarked cars. They were parked between two buildings and behind a row of pine trees, well hidden from view.

"Keep it short," Zach instructed her, gently untucking her hair from the collar of her jacket. "Let Allison do most of the talking. Just enough to incriminate herself on tape. Then get out of there."

He still wasn't ready to admit that Gilbert would keep his word to her. But she had no doubt about who was meeting her tonight. "I'll be all right."

Zach met her gaze. "I'm counting on it."

She wanted to tell him how much she loved him. That he was the man who mattered most to her in the world, not Gilbert. But this wasn't the time or the place, not with those other cops close enough to hear her.

Thunder rumbled in the sky, threatening a downpour at any moment. Gracie suppressed a shiver, though the night air was still hot and humid.

Sergeant Hayes walked up to them. "Are you ready?"

Gracie nodded, her throat too tight to speak.

"It's not too late to change your mind," Zach said. "You don't need to do this."

"Yes," she replied softly. "I do."

He stared at her for a moment, then gave a jerky nod, turning away as she climbed into her car.

Gracie switched on the engine, then pulled onto the street, feeling more vulnerable than ever now that she was on her own. Zach and the other officers would move closer to the warehouse once she was inside. She just hoped she didn't blow it.

Lightning flashed when she reached the warehouse, as if warning her away. She shook herself, realizing she was letting Zach's fears for her safety infect her. This was Gilbert, after all. Her best friend. The man she'd always been able to trust.

The rain spattering on her windshield multiplied and she knew if she didn't get out of the car soon, she'd get soaked. Taking a deep breath, she tipped her chin toward the wire and said, "I'm going in."

She could feel the wire move when she reached for her purse and hoped she hadn't dislodged it. Then she opened the car door and made a run for the warehouse. Rain dampened her hair and eyelashes, blurring her vision.

The door opened before she got there, Gilbert standing on the other side. She breathed a sigh of relief that he'd been the one to meet her.

"Hey, you made it," he said. "I was starting to worry."

"Sorry, I'm late." Gracie wiped the moisture out of her eyes.

"No, problem." Gilbert smiled. "I knew you'd come."

He trusted her, not knowing she was wired and that the police were only a short distance away. But she wasn't doing this to trap him, only to help him. If Zach *was* right and Gilbert was more involved than she believed, he'd need all the help he could get.

"Did you bring the tape?" he asked.

She pushed her damp bangs off her forehead. "No."

He frowned. "But Gracie, I need—"

"I found the key," she interjected.

Gilbert froze. "What?"

As soon as she saw his reaction, something inside of her withered. Zach was right. Gilbert wasn't an innocent dupe in this case. "Inside the video cassette. The key to your old safe-deposit box at the bank."

He rubbed one hand over the back of his neck, obviously buying some time to think. "So…do you have the key with you now?"

"No." She didn't elaborate, wanting him to explain exactly what was going on, to make her understand how the boy she'd known so well could have changed so much in the past ten years.

Gilbert met her gaze. "Don't look at me like that, Gracie. You don't know what it's been like."

"Then tell me."

He got up and started to pace across the dusty concrete floor. "We both had such big plans back in high school. I was going to get a full scholarship to MIT and get a job at NASA. Rub elbows with the astronauts…" Gilbert turned to face her, bitterness turning down the corners of his mouth. "Well, we both know that neither of our dreams came true. I ended up doing IT work like a million other guys, barely making ends meet."

"But you went to Boston College and got a degree," she said, amazed at the self-pity she heard in his voice. "That's a great school."

"Yeah, but I bombed out with the women there just like I did in high school. *None* of my dreams ever came true. Nobody ever really cared about me except you, Gracie."

She rose to her feet, wishing he'd confided all of this to her sooner, before he'd gotten in so deep. "I still care about you, Gilbert. That's why I want to help you now. It's time to turn yourself into the police. You know I'll stand by you all the way."

One of the cardboard boxes stacked around them tumbled to the floor, startling them both. Gracie looked over to see Allison appear from behind the stack, a gun in her hand and an implacable expression on her thin face.

"That isn't going to happen, is it, Gilbert?" Allison said, moving beside him.

He looked between the two of them, clearly torn. "Allison, this isn't necessary. Gracie's not the enemy."

"The way I see it, she is." Allison's cheeks grew mottled with anger.

Gilbert shook his head. "Gracie's just a friend. You're the only woman I love."

"Then why did you send her the tape with the damn key?" Allison exclaimed. "You've delayed leaving this hick town until you could explain everything to her. Now she's the only one who can stop us." She trained the gun on Gracie. "Unless I stop her first."

"Look, I—" Gracie began, wanting to defuse the situation.

But Allison wasn't going to give her the chance. "Say good night, Gracie."

Then she pulled the trigger.

16

ZACH'S HEART LURCHED in his chest when he heard the gunshot echo over the headset.

Gracie.

Fear clutched at his throat and cramped the muscles in his gut. He tore off the headset, then raced toward the warehouse, his legs as heavy as lead.

Why had he ever let her go in there alone? He'd known it was dangerous. Known she didn't understand how desperation could drive people to do something crazy. Now Gracie had paid the price for his bad judgment.

Voices and footsteps sounded behind him, but he didn't take the time to turn around. He knew the other officers had no idea why he'd taken off on a dead run for the warehouse.

When he reached the building, he made himself stop, knowing he had a duty to protect the officers even as he ached to be with Gracie.

"Shots fired," he said hoarsely, pulling his gun from his shoulder holster.

They followed suit, then took the standard positions for a raid. Zach led the way to the door, moving faster than procedure allowed but too desperate to find Gracie to care.

If he lost her...

He swallowed hard, knowing he wouldn't be able to function if he even considered that possibility.

He kicked open the door, shouting, "Police!"

The first thing he saw was the blood running on the uneven concrete floor. His gut clenched and a small moan escaped from the back of his throat. His gaze followed the stream of blood until he saw the body lying on the floor.

It wasn't Gracie.

Relief made his knees buckle, but he managed to remain upright as he hurried to her side. She sat on the floor with Gilbert's head cradled in her lap. The guy was alive, but woozy. From his vantage point, Zach couldn't tell where or how badly he'd been shot.

Tears glistened on Gracie's cheeks as she looked up at him. "I love you, Zach. I almost didn't get the chance to tell you that. I love you."

"Shh," he murmured, emotion welling up inside of him. He fought it back, determined to stay professional.

She started trembling as the other officers attended to Gilbert, one of them calling dispatch for an ambulance.

Hayes arrived at his side. "What happened?"

Gracie sucked in a deep breath. "Allison showed up and pulled a gun. She was going to shoot me, but Gilbert dived in the way. He saved my life."

Zach's chest tightened until he had trouble drawing breath. He'd come so close to losing her, the only person in the world who really mattered to him.

"Where did Allison go?" Hayes asked Gracie.

"She panicked when Gilbert went down and ran out the back door."

Hayes waved his arm at his men to go into pursuit, then looked at Zach. "You take care of her. I'll handle the other two."

Zach shrugged out of his jacket and placed it over Gracie's shoulders. She was shaking violently now. He picked her up in his arms, never wanting to let her go.

"I thought you were shot. I thought…" He let his voice trail off, unable to form the words that had almost shattered his heart.

Sirens sounded in the distance as she wrapped her hands around his neck. "I'm all right, Zach. Really. Just a little shaky."

His grasp tightened around her. "You're in shock," he told her, moving toward the door. "You need to see a doctor."

"I'm fine," she protested.

But this time, he wasn't going to be dissuaded. He forced himself to hand her over to the care of the paramedics. They took her vital signs, then placed her on a stretcher and put her in the second ambulance. The first one containing Gilbert had already left, the siren screaming into the night.

"We got her," Hayes said, coming up behind him. "Allison Webb is in custody. Looks like you closed the case, Detective Maddox."

He nodded, too choked up to speak. This was the danger of letting someone into your heart. He'd let Gracie in and almost lost her. Now part of him understood his mother's choice to wall herself off from the world. It just hurt too damn much.

Maybe it was time for him to make that choice as well. For good.

THE NEXT DAY, Gracie walked into Between the Covers to find Trina packing books into one of the many boxes scattered around the room.

"What are you doing here?" Trina asked. "Shouldn't you be home in bed?"

That was the last place she wanted to be. Her bed held too many memories of Zach. She could still smell his aftershave on her pillow, making sleep impossible for the few hours she'd been able to rest last night.

After the doctor had declared her perfectly healthy, Gracie had stayed at the hospital long past midnight, until she was assured Gilbert would be all right. He'd suffered a superficial gunshot wound in the gluteus muscle. Or as he'd wryly put it, his big butt.

She'd expected Zach to show up at the hospital, but one of the officers told her that he was at the police station arranging for Gilbert's extradition and trying to explain events to his irate captain back in Boston.

Though she'd tried calling him on his cell phone, Zach hadn't picked up. Maybe he was avoiding her. Gracie didn't want to believe it, but she couldn't come up with any other explanation.

Had her declaration of love scared him off?

After coming within a few inches of that bullet, Gracie had been so grateful for the chance to tell him her feelings she hadn't even considered his reaction. But she wouldn't take the words back. She loved Zach Maddox and nothing would ever change that.

"I'm perfectly fine," Gracie said, pulling an empty box toward her. "And ready to get some work done."

"Good, because I have some news."

"What?"

"Remember that great location Paul told you about? Well, he sealed the deal yesterday. It's downtown, in the same building as The Bean Tree."

Gracie tried to feel excited for Trina's sake, but inside she just felt numb. "That's great."

"It's more than great," Trina exclaimed. "It's fantastic! The Bean Tree is the most popular coffeehouse in Kendall. We'll have a huge customer base ready and waiting for us."

Despite Gracie's lethargy, she found Trina's enthusiasm contagious. Every part of her life was going well—except one. But if she couldn't be with the man she loved, then what was the point?

"Even better," Trina continued, "Paul's made arrangements with the owner to construct an open archway between the two businesses. That will guarantee us a great customer flow."

Gracie thought about her Aunt Fran and knew her legacy would live on. Now it was time for Gracie to begin her own legacy. "How would you like a promotion, Trina?"

Trina looked up from her box. "What are you talking about?"

"I've decided to go to law school this fall in Austin and I need someone to run the bookstore. Are you interested in the job?"

To Gracie's surprise, tears sprang into Trina's eyes. "This is too much. First I get Paul and now I get to run the bookstore. That's been my dream for as long as I can remember."

"A dream that's going to come with a lot of hard work," Gracie reminded her. "I'll be busy taking classes and studying again, so I probably won't be in much. Are you sure you don't mind handling all of this by yourself?"

"Positive," Trina replied, packing books with a renewed vigor. "In fact, I've got some great ideas for the new store. I'll outline them for your approval and—"

"Not necessary," Gracie interjected. "Paul's a partner in the business now. His approval is good enough for me."

"Me, too." She laughed. "Especially since I'm sleeping with the boss."

Her joy for her friend's happiness was tinged with envy. "So everything's working out between you two?"

"Oh, Gracie," Trina said with a sigh. "I've never been happier in my entire life. Paul may seem quiet around here, but once he starts talking he's spellbinding. The man knows everything. He's just... wonderful."

She laughed. "And it only took you three years to figure it out."

"Paul told me I was worth the wait," Trina chimed, and then her smile turned mischievous. "Of course, if I'd known how good he is in bed, I never would have held out for so long."

Gracie smiled, knowing no man could ever compare to Zach. Or perhaps it was her love for him that made him so perfect in bed. She just wished those feelings had been able to sustain them *out* of bed.

They packed books until noon, saving Aunt Fran's Harlequin collection in the back of the store for after lunch. Trina left to meet Paul at a downtown restaurant, but Gracie chose to run over to Temptation for a quick order to go.

When she returned to the bookstore, she wondered why she'd even bothered to buy lunch. She didn't have much of an appetite, even though Cat had told her that Laine and Tess would be back in town next week and the four of them would be getting together. Cat didn't say why she'd planned the mystery meeting and Gracie didn't want to get her hopes up.

She wasn't ready to say goodbye to Tess and Laine and Cat. They, along with Trina, were the sisters she'd never had, the only women who really understood her. But all their lives were changing now. They each had their own dream to pursue.

Her mind drifted back to Zach. There was still no word from him and Gracie was beginning to give up hope. For all she knew, he could be on a plane to Boston by now and she'd never see him again.

She set the takeout bag from Temptation on her desk, deciding to save it for later. Maybe she'd have an appetite after she'd packed up some more books. But the sound of footsteps in one of the aisles told her she'd have to wait on a customer first.

Gracie swallowed a sigh, wishing she'd locked the door before running over to Temptation to pick up her lunch. She walked over and flipped the sign on the door to read Closed, knowing she needed some time alone.

But first she had to get rid of her latest customer. She just hoped it wasn't a browser, one of those people who spent hours hanging around reading the merchandise.

Gracie moved toward the aisle. "May I help you…"

The words died on her lips when she saw Zach standing there. He looked dangerously sexy with the dark shadow of whiskers on his jaw. Though he'd showered and changed from the day before, her intuition told her he'd been up all night.

"I hope so," he replied. "I'm looking for a story with a happy ending."

She swallowed hard, too stunned to think straight. "What kind of story?"

"Oh, it's definitely a romance. I don't know the title, but the main characters are an aspiring law student and a Kendall city cop."

Hope mingled with the fear that she might be reading him all wrong. "I don't understand."

"Don't you?" He moved beside her, taking both

of her hands in his own. "I love you, Gracie Dawson. Simple as that. It just took me a while to figure it out. Cops are dense that way sometimes—and stubborn."

"I noticed," she breathed, telling herself this wasn't a dream. It was real. Beautifully, wonderfully real.

He reached out to caress her cheek. "Do you think you can stand having a dense, stubborn guy like me around for the next forty or fifty years?"

"Is that all?" she asked, joy bubbling up inside of her. "I was hoping for a lot longer."

"I'm glad you feel that way." His gaze softened on her as he moved closer. "Because I've just accepted a job with the Kendall Police Department. I want to be as close to you as possible for as long as possible."

"Oh, Zach," she exclaimed, wanting to laugh and cry at the same time. But part of her still held back. She didn't want him to have any regrets. "Are you absolutely sure about this? What if you miss Boston? What if you don't like living in Kendall? What if you're bored—"

He silenced all her worst scenarios with a kiss that convinced her that life wasn't going to be boring at all.

When he finally pulled back, she looked into his dark brown eyes and saw the promise of more happiness than she'd ever dared to dream of.

"I love you," Zach said hoarsely. Then he pressed his hard length against her with a groan of desire. "I want you."

"Then what are you waiting for?" Gracie whispered, pulling him to her for another kiss. This one was even hotter than before, with an urgency that neither of them could deny.

Gracie leaned against a bookshelf as Zach's fingers began to work the buttons of her blouse. She helped him, pulling her blouse open so she could feel his hands on her skin.

Zach obliged, dropping his head to her breasts and suckling them through the thin silk of her bra as his fingers lifted her skirt past her waist.

Then his hands were sliding into her panties, pulling them downward. She arched against the solid oak behind her as he dipped his fingers inside of her, finding her wet and ready.

Gracie heard the rip of a condom package, followed by the rustle of clothing. Then he was finally inside her. She moaned at the exquisite sensation, wanting it to last forever.

But it only got better.

She grasped his shoulders as he lifted her legs on either side of his hips. He filled her completely, making her cry out in ecstasy as he began to move. The bookshelf quaked behind her, but all she could feel was Zach. His strength. His desire. His love.

His cry of satisfaction ripped through the air, compelling her own as her body clenched and rocked with pleasure. The motion caused all the paperback books to tumble off the shelves above, raining down on them as they found their completion.

When she finally caught her breath, Gracie gazed at all the Harlequin Temptations scattered around them. "Here you go, Zach. Now you can take your pick of happy endings."

Zach looked at the books surrounding them, then met her gaze, a forever kind of love shining in his eyes. "I pick you."

The
Temptation
Years
1984–2005

<u>Autographs</u>

Temptation —
Thanks for the memories
Barbara Daly

Temptation is and always
will be home. The line
and its readers gave me
my start. I love you all!
Carly Phillips

Temptation always had the heroines I
wanted to be - and the heroes I wanted
to have!
Cindi Myers

Thanks for the memories,
Temptation! And thanks
especially for putting me
in touch with so many
wonderful readers. I'll miss you.
Cara Summers

I'll miss our steamy, nights and laughs, although!
Jule McBride

I ♡ Temptations!
I made my Harlequin
debut there & found
some of my 'fave
authors between
Temptation covers.
Temptresses RULE! ☺
Dawn Atkins

My dear Temptation,
What can I say? You've
given me some wonderful reads,
launched my career, and introduced
me to a whole slew of new friends.
You had a fabulous run and I'll miss you!

Love,
Julie Kenner

It is with great sadness I say goodbye
to Temptation. So many wonderful
stories... So many great authors. Thanks
to editors Brenda Chin and Jennifer Green
for giving me a home, and to the
Temptresses for making me feel so
welcome!

All my best,

Jill Monroe

Dear Temptation,
Thanks for giving Thea
Nuse Jane a chance to be
"just a little bit naughty."
Darlene Schacht

Dear Temptation,
You were the first Harlequin line
I fell in love with as a reader,
and the line I felt honored
to break into as an author.
Colleen Collins

Thanks for my ten tempting years!
Heather MacAllister
June 1995 - June 2005

For all the friends I've made
and stories I've loved-- It was
my pleasure to be led into Temptation
Jacquie D'Alessandro

Thanks for giving me my
start! I'll always be
a "Temptation" writer.
Kate Hoffmann

Dear Temptation-

What a run! As a reader,
I learned anything is
possible if you approach
life with a little sass.

Heck, I learned the same
as a writer.
Here's to sass!
Julie Elizabeth
Leto

"Temptation" was right There at the
start of SEXY and HOT. She'll be
remembered with love and a
quickened pulse by
Barbara Delinsky

My love and undying gratitude
to my readers. I couldn't have
enjoyed seventeen fabulous years
at Temptation without you!
Kristine Rolofson

Temptation will always
have a home on my bookshelf!
KRISTIN GABRIEL

First Kiss. First lover. First book.
I'll never forget the Temptation!
Smooches,
Colleen ♡

My keeper shelf is stuffed
full of Temptation stories
and I've loved every month
of this awesome line! Thanks
for all the great reading :)
Joanne Rock

Writing for the Temptation line
helped me to find my voice as
a writer. I'm proud to be
forever linked to this line as
a Temptress! Stephanie Bond

Happy retirement,
Temptation!
You've brought me so
much joy and laughter
through the years. It's
hard to watch you go.
- Wendy Etherington

For years, Temptations were the books I loved to read. Becoming a Temptress was a dream come true and forged lasting friendships with both authors and readers. Thank you, Temptation, for the fun, laughter, and good times!

Janelle Denison

Not only did Temptation give me my start, it also gave me some of the greatest friends of my life. I'll always be honored to have been a Temptress!

Leslie Kelly

Thanks to Harlequin — You let your writers spread their wings and fly. We're touched the sky.

Sandra Chastain

Thank you, Temptation, for giving me special friends I'll value for a lifetime. The camaraderie and talent within the line, and the readers who gave it popularity, made writing for Temptation a very special time in my life. I'll miss the fun more than I can say.

Lori Foster

My very first book was a Temptation, so the line will always hold a special place in my heart.

I wish all the talented authors, brilliant editors and, most of all, the faithful readers all the best for the future.

Always a Temptress!
Nancy Warren

From getting that first call for CALL ME on national televisio to being a part of the line's 15th Anniversary... thanks, Temptation, for all of the memories!! Alison Kent

There's nothing like diving into a short, totally fun story — I have only the best memories of writing for Temptation.
Carla Neggers

Temptation Romances taught me to believe. Not only in the power of love, but also in the power of being a woman. So being published in the line was the ultimate expression of all the things I learned from the line, independence, belief in myself, and faith that success on every level was within my grasp. Thank you HQ for giving women strong, sexy role models to show them the way!

Mara Fox

Hey, sweet Temptation! What a kick
hanging out with you. Thanks for the
memories! X X O O Vicki Lewis Thompson

True love stories never
have endings —
Friends 4-ever!
Jen & Tom
aka
Toni Lorring

JoAnn Ross

I can resist everything
but Temptations!!
Kathleen
O'Reilly

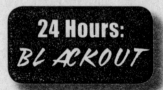

presents

the final installment of

THREE WAY WAGER

*The Reilly triplets bet they could go
ninety days without sex. Hmm.*

THE LAST
REILLY STANDING

by Maureen Child

(SD #1664, available July 2005)

Aidan Reilly was determined to win the bet
he'd made with his brothers. Three months
without sex meant one thing: spend *a lot* of
time with his best gal pal Terry Evans. She had
given up on love long ago because the pain
just wasn't worth it. Then…temptation proved
to be too much. The last Reilly standing had
lost the bet, but could he win the girl?

Available at your favorite retail outlet.